THE PERSIAN OVEN
and
CALIFORNIA EXIT

James White is an American writer, whose
poetry and short stories have appeared in
numerous magazines in the USA. He was
until quite recently a Visiting Professor at the
University of Texas in Dallas, and now
teaches in Mobile, Alabama. This is his second book to be published in the UK; his first
novel, BIRDSONG, was published in 1985.

James White

THE PERSIAN OVEN
and
CALIFORNIA EXIT

Methuen

First published in Great Britain 1987
by Methuen London Ltd
11 New Fetter Lane, London EC4P 4EE
The Persian Oven was first published in USA 1983
by Imperial Press, a division of OMK & Co
The Persian Oven copyright © 1983, 1987 by James White
California Exit copyright © 1987 by James White

Printed and bound in Great Britain
by Richard Clay Ltd, Bungay, Suffolk

British Library Cataloguing in Publication Data

White, James P.
    The Persian oven; and, California exit.
    I. Title
    813'.54[F]   PS3573.H4727
    ISBN 0–413–15050–X
    ISBN 0–413–15060–7 Pbk

For Chris, Don, and Jules

Contents

The Persian Oven

February

Ben pressed the elevator button for the eighteenth floor, stepped back, and watched the numbers light as the floors passed effortlessly. He rubbed his fingers against the brass fastener of his briefcase. When the chrome doors opened, he hurried along the hallway, turning right toward the black marble entrance of Wynn and Eichman, literary agents.

Inside, the foyer resembled a movie set more than an office. A carved gilt mirror, hung on a grape-coloured wall, held his reflection. The carpet was deep, more boldly patterned than the hallway. Under the chandelier, a receptionist sat at a high-legged table and held a phone at her ear. When she glanced up, she raised her eyebrows.

'I have an appointment with Liz Schorer,' he said.

'Yes. Would you have a seat while I buzz her secretary?' She still did not recognize him.

The single chair across from the mirror had upholstered arms, curved legs, and was red velvet. He glanced at himself in the mirror against the fake richness, then at the bookcase of new novels beneath it.

'Hi Ben,' Liz's secretary said, her jeans as slim as she was, her blouse open, silky at her small breasts. She could have been on roller skates she walked so smoothly.

He followed her past the receptionist, along a hallway. Then he saw Liz, the door open to the large office. She was using the telephone, and motioned to him. Would he come on in?

He sat quietly on a white sofa that matched hers and listened as she finished her call.

She hung up. 'I'm sorry,' she said. 'Would you like coffee?'

'No, thank you.' He unfastened the briefcase while she watched, and took out the typed sheets. Listen, he thought, I don't think you're going to like this. He noticed that she smiled reassuringly. 'I've worked out an idea that I think would be interesting for a feature.' He hesitated and she lighted a cigarette, then nodded. 'Did you know that the last emperor of China became a communist prisoner and later a gardener who worked for the Republic? He has a fascinating story.'

'No, I didn't,' she said.

'My plot's about him,' Ben said.

'Nobody cares about China,' she said. She sat up from the wide pillow. 'Is it about China?'

How could he deny it? 'But China's wonderful,' he said. 'This boy became emperor at three, lived until he was twenty-one in a palace called the Violet Enclosure right in the heart of Peking. Can you imagine being in a violet enclosure? He didn't go outside of the palace until he was grown. Then he was a traitor to the Chinese in . . .'

'China is out. People aren't interested. If I did sell it for you – and I couldn't – if it got produced and was shown, not twenty-five people in the whole country would watch. The producer would literally strangle you and me.'

He put the sheet, single-spaced with detail, to the bottom of the stack. 'Well,' he said, 'give me a minute.'

She smoothed the sofa cushion beside her, considerately.

'Do you read much?' he asked.

'I read *all* the time. I almost don't have a social life because I read at night. I stayed up until two this morning with a beautiful new novel. I'm sure I can sell it for a major feature.'

He bet she could. He didn't want to hear any more about it. He thought that he was ready for another crack at it and that she was in a hurry. He coughed first, then glanced at her. 'This one is about a husband who stays home and keeps the baby while his wife works.'

'Yes,' she said.

'The husband can't find a job, but the wife has one. He's thrown into taking the kid to the park where he sits with the mothers; he buys formula and fixes it, takes the kid shopping. I've written a synopsis.' He handed her the typed pages. Keep talking, he told himself, pitch it. You have to convince *her*.

She held the pages in the better light and read. 'It's soft but not terrible,' she said. 'I know of four projects like it that are in production now. But it's a possibility.'

'And I have a third. It's for Disney. I've written it down, too.'

Oh well, he thought, waiting as she skimmed. She did read fast. He felt as if he were listening for a school bell to ring, saying he could go. He looked at his watch.

'Umm,' she said. 'I can see it's for Disney. But it has too much sex.'

'Fred Lalley there told me they wanted something more daring. I purposely added the sex.'

'He's been saying that for years,' she said. 'And have you seen what they've bought?'

'Well let me ask you something,' Ben said. 'Can I? I don't want to take up your time, but you could really help me.'

'I'll be glad to.' Liz raised the coffee past her knees on the sofa, to her lips. She blew softly to cool it.

'What should I look for in a topic?'

She shook her head quickly. 'Oh I couldn't answer that. I'm not a writer. And I wouldn't want to interfere with a writer's creativity. You're a good writer, a novelist. I don't say that to put you down.'

'But tell me, what movies have you seen that you've liked? That would help.'

'Oh very few,' she said. She wrinkled her brow, then touched her nail to her mouth. 'I don't want to mislead you. I don't like any one in particular that is showing now.'

He nodded, waiting a second, his typed plots like waste paper in his hands. He took the typed sheets she held too, then stuck them all in the briefcase.

13

'But how do you know what people want to watch?' he asked.

Her face changed subtly. Her nose slightly turned, higher; her eyes just darted, first at him, then back. 'Because that's my business,' she said. 'I get asked that all the time.' She took a moment to smile at him. 'Let's make another appointment for two weeks from now,' she said. 'I think you get closer every time. I really do.' She walked toward her desk, the sheer curtains a négligé across Hollywood. Her lips parted, her mauve lipstick glistening.

'Thank you,' he said.

Outside the building, he took a deep breath and walked toward a restaurant-bar he had seen across the street. He had parked several blocks away, in front of a house that was being remodelled, just past the Beverly Hills city limit sign. He waited at the light, then crossed and entered the restaurant. The darkness contrasted with the sunlight outside. He sat at a small marble table that wobbled.

'I'd like a scotch and soda,' he told the waitress. He looked about for a moment. The restaurant was crowded with successful people in jeans, a few in dark suits, women with their hair tangled like lions in hay. He sort of sank in the soft chair, and in a few minutes, began to enjoy the drink. Heavens, he thought, and in that moment, gave Hollywood back to Liz.

A half hour later, he pressed on the gas pedal of his Toyota, palm trees along the boulevard sweeping by. He put thoughts of movie ideas in the far back of his mind. What he had to do now was clear. Liz wasn't going to try to sell anything for him that she didn't think would sell. Why should she even if she could? And really, he didn't care if his ideas would *sell*. It made him feel ridiculous around her.

You're going to have to get a job, he told himself.

He passed a Mercedes, then a Lancia. Sunlight gleamed against the Westwood highrise ahead. Good, he thought, I'd rather.

2

Jobs in the *L.A. Times* want ads abounded like healthy rabbits. Ben had never turned to the section before that afternoon. When he did, it was like opening cans from the grocery store and sniffing them. Why, anything in the world was a possibility for someone who wanted to work. Of course he ruled out taking something foreign, such as going to an unpronounceable town in Saudi Arabia where technical writers were desperately needed. He couldn't do criminal or physically dangerous work or a job that required knowledge he didn't have, such as an electrician or a plumber.

He could look at most all the openings, however, free to pick and choose. He had to support Alice and Jules, but for a while did it matter to him, how? He didn't think so. The job he looked for was temporary.

He ran his pink finger down the page. He felt somewhat giddy, like Pooh, freed from getting stuck in the opening to the rabbit's den. The situation offered a pocket of freedom that had come to his mind like that.

If you want to find a job, he thought, first you should be willing to work hard. In principle, he should be willing to do any honest job, no matter how menial. Wasn't he? Yes.

And he should look at the ads closely, because each one contained a chance that no one knew about. If he tried, he might learn printing, getting his fingers stained with blue ink, or insurance selling and wear a coat and tie every day, or waiting tables to see if he got big tips like he gave. Or he could learn information that people needed such as in a computer programmer training job. But he didn't want to do what he already had: teach.

He made a check mark by a number in the want ad section under *B – Bakers. Manager. Excellent salary. Immediate openings. Call MU3-4100.* Well go on, he told himself. Nothing's going to happen until you pick up the phone. You could sit here all day. He picked up the receiver and dialled the number.

'Le Champs,' a woman answered.

'Is this the bakery?' he asked. 'I'm calling about the *Times* ad.'

'For a baker?' Her throaty voice was excited with some confusion that must be going on.

He hesitated, tempted to say yes. He would like to learn how to bake. But how could a bakery hire him if he didn't know how already? 'For the manager's job,' he said.

'We're interviewing today and tomorrow,' she said. 'Would you like to make an appointment? Have you managed a bakery before?'

'I've taught in college,' Ben said. 'I have a lot of experience teaching. I'm interested in changing fields.'

'Just a minute,' she said. 'Let me ask Abe.' She covered the phone while he waited.

'If you'd like to talk to Abe Goldstein, I'll make you an appointment for tomorrow.'

'Will you work at Le Champs?' he asked.

'My name's Brenda' she said. 'I work with Abe in starting new stores. How about one o'clock?'

He took down the address, 120 South Westwood Boulevard, then thanked her. It wasn't far from Santa Monica where he lived. He looked back and tore out the ad.

The want ads were listed under headings. Under teaching, there were immediate openings in parochial schools, mostly elementary. If there was unusual teaching, he thought, then hastily skipped the entire column. Back to the first then. After baker were bartender, beautician, cashier, cook, cutter, dye worker. The number of things he didn't know how to do was growing. He glanced at a bartender's job, located in a Westwood hotel. Experienced. The listings themselves were too succinct, uninformative. Something in business, he thought, as if he were reading a menu. He carefully ran his finger down the page. At the end of the list, under 'w', he spotted 'Writer', and under that, 'Ghost writer needed to assist business executive writing book. 457–1112. Mr Freeman.' Go on, he thought. Don't hesitate.

He picked up the phone and dialled.

'Union Gold Corporation.'

'I'm calling Mr Freeman,' Ben said.

'One moment please.'

The two-second wait let him picture the office: in a glass highrise, a view of buildings spread out before Mr Freeman. Him in a leather chair, leaning back, the telephone to his ear.

'Yes?'

'This is Ben Escobio, I'm calling about your ad for a ghost writer.'

'You, too?' Mr Freeman asked. 'Writers have been coming out of the woodwork.'

'I'm not surprised. There are a lot of people trying. You should be careful who you hire.'

'How should I be careful?'

'If you want a good book you have to hire someone who writes well. You should be sure to read their work.'

'I think you're right,' Mr Freeman said.

'I'd be glad to leave a book of mine by, if you want to see it. I can bring it this afternoon.'

'I'd like to very much. Let me give you the address.'

Ben nodded, then, as he wrote it down, looked out the window. Mr Freeman's office was in the building he looked at from the balcony. It was a dark glass structure, only two blocks away.

'Do you know where . . .' Mr Freeman began.

'It's close to where I live,' Ben said. In all of L.A., he thought, he's that close. 'I know exactly where it is,' he said.

When he hung up, he sat back in the dinette chair. He looked pleased at the marked pages and the torn out ads. There were nice x's and boxes around what looked interesting. He glanced at his watch: 5 p.m. He had a head start, and from only five calls, had two interviews.

At five until one the next afternoon, he shut the Toyota door and walked across Westwood traffic to number 120. The front of the building didn't look like a bakery. The curb was lined with Mercedes, all of them dirty. He entered the glass doors and looked for someone to ask about Le Champs.

Inside, a cluster of foreigners stood talking, boiling over loudly, most of them in suits and white shirts without ties. A reception desk, just past the glass door, was empty. He didn't understand the langauge that was being spoken.

'Are you looking for Abe Goldstein?' someone asked suddenly. 'He's interviewing upstairs.'

What kind of place is this, he asked himself, his polished shoes against the new carpeting on the steps. At the landing he stood before an open office with two small desks, both occupied.

'Are you Ben?' the woman asked, her voice suddenly Brenda. She wore owl-sized glasses, and her hair was everywhere to her shoulders. It had been brushed, but was like wire. She was sort of pretty. 'Just a minute and Abe will see you. Come on in.'

Abe Goldstein sat at the desk and used the telephone. His sleeves were rolled up; the buttons on his white shirt threatened to pop at his stomach.

'He won't be a minute,' Brenda said. 'When you asked me if I'd be working at Le Champs I was startled. I work for Abe in Philadelphia.'

'Shhh,' Abe said, his finger across his mouth. He looked as

if he weighed over two hundred and fifty, with much of it in his shoulders and arms. His hands were big, laid out on the desk, his fingers nervously rubbing together. He was over fifty.

'Don't pay any attention to him,' Brenda whispered. 'He's really very nice. Would you like coffee? Just speak low.'

'Where is the bakery?' Ben asked. He liked Brenda's friendliness. He ignored Abe, waiting for him to finish.

'They're not open. And there are two. Did you see the man who left just as you got here? He's the new quick pastry chef at Westwood. You wouldn't believe the head baker. He's here from Sweden.'

Abe hung up the phone and scooted the desk chair back. He obviously was about to say something brusque that no one wanted him to.

'I'm glad to meet you,' Ben said. 'I hope I'm not wasting your time. I know I don't have the experience' you're expecting, but I've managed a lot of people.' He handed Abe the data sheet he brought. 'I'd like to tell you about myself.'

Abe held up a finger, meaning for him to stop. Abe said nothing and read the data sheet. Then he took a moment, looking him directly in the eyes. Finally, he spoke. 'You have experience managing students,' he said. 'It's a lot easier to handle a student you can give an F to, than a drunk baker. And ninety-nine per cent of them are alcoholics.' He puffed on the cigarette. 'Tell me. What comes to mind when you think of a bakery?'

'I think of how good the bread smells.'

'But what do you picture? A half mile line of counters with a little old lady who walks a block looking for a nickel doughnut? Le Champs isn't like that.' He leaned over closer, his voice louder. 'It's a new concept that's going to make a million.'

'I'd like to make a million dollars,' Ben şaid.

'You're not going to do it managing bakeries.'

'I might decide to start my own.'

'And I'm supposed to hire the competition?'

'Abe!' Brenda said. 'Be nice.'

'You can make a lot of money though. You could make thirty-five or forty thousand, more with the percentage. Then you could buy a franchise from me. These stores are going to be nationwide in two years.'

'So you sell them all over the country?'

'I own the franchise. These I'll sell you for one dollar. You pay for setting up the business and it costs you a buck to start. Do you have a dollar? Give it to me.'

'Then you get a percentage?'

'Sure.' Abe straightened in the chair, took out another cigarette and before he lighted it, continued. 'I'll be honest with you. I like educated people. The man who owns these bakeries was educated in Europe. Me, I'm self-educated.'

'Julian was educated in France,' Brenda said. 'Julian Alexander owns the bakeries.'

'Julian is one of the last gentlemen anywhere,' Abe said. 'He's a man of his word. You don't write anything down with Julian. Everything is done like in Iran – by handshake.'

'There's one thing I should tell you,' Ben said. 'You can trust me.'

'I think I'm a good enough judge to tell if I can trust somebody. Can I, Brenda?'

She nodded, her chin resting on both palms. 'I think so, Abe.'

'I'm sure you are,' Ben said. 'And I meant that *you* could always trust me.'

'For instance I wouldn't worry about trusting you. You're a professional in your field. But I'd be making a terrific mistake to hire you and have you quit in a month, which is what you would do.'

'No, I wouldn't.'

'You tell me that. But managing bakeries isn't easy. Look at these hands.' He spread them out, fingernails up, then palms first. 'Do you think that they look like this because I haven't worked? You think I don't know the business from the bottom up?'

'Oh Abe,' Brenda said.

'Before I'd hire you, I would want you to promise me you wouldn't quit for three months. In three or four months I'd get my money back on you. Not if you tried it two weeks and quit. I'd have to fly back from Philadelphia, and I'd wring your neck. It's expensive to open a store. Julian already has over a million dollars in these two. I'd have to have your word.'

'I wouldn't quit.' Come on, he thought. Give me a chance.

'Your job would be to run these stores as if you owned them. You'd call me every morning in Philadelphia and whenever you needed me.' Abe held up the data sheet and reread it. Finally he looked up. 'Ben, you know my boy wants to be a writer. He graduates in two months and will be going to college next year. I tell him, you can be a writer and major in anything you want. You don't have to major in English. Go into business.'

'That's all right,' Ben said.

'So now if I hire you I go back to Philadelphia and say, "Well your daddy's hiring college teachers of writing now. So what's so great about it? Your teacher is going into business."'

'I think he should be a writer,' Ben said. 'If he wants to be and you don't let him, you'll regret it.'

'Let me tell you. I admire writers. I would give my left arm to the armpit if he grew up to write a good book. I am behind him one hundred per cent but it doesn't hurt to put a little temptation in his path.'

'It's good you appreciate him.'

'I love him. I don't want him to make a mistake already. So tell me, what do you think of being manager? What I've got in mind is – we were going to hire two managers. But if we hired you to manage both stores, we should be able to save money and to give you more than we planned. How much do you expect to make?'

'Well, I'd like-uh-forty thousand.'

'I'd like the moon. What would you take?'

'I'd rather you make an offer.'

'You understand you wouldn't be working for me. I'd pay you nothing and let you get experience. Julian came here from Iran about a year ago. He's a very cultured man. I think he'd like you.' Abe tapped his fingers against the desktop. 'Julian wants everything first class,' he said. 'Everything. You wouldn't have any problem with him. Money is no question. When could you start?'

'I'd like a few days if I could.' He suddenly thought of a vacation, easily affordable with his new job. Maybe Capistrano. He would buy Jules something really special. And for Alice –

'It'd have to be tomorrow,' Abe said. 'The day after, I go to Philly, but someone has to be here in charge. Could you start tomorrow?'

'Yes.'

'I'll call you by eight tonight either way. I'll give a salary then. All right?'

'Fine,' Ben said, standing up. He shook Abe's hand then Brenda's. 'Where are the bakeries?' he asked.

'Have you seen the building with the new blue canopy in Westwood?' Brenda asked. 'That's one.'

'I have,' he said. And going downstairs, he thought that he liked the canopy and the building very much. He would drive by. He saw that the men downstairs were Iranians and he wondered which was Julian. Were they talking about the revolution? He nodded toward the boy who now sat at the desk, then he left through the glass double doors.

He drove the short blocks to Westwood Village and turned up Bexley, looking for the building. He couldn't remember what street it was on. At a three-corner intersection, he went right, saw a red brick office building across from him and at the end of the street, the bakery. It was one storey, a picture window in front, and bright blue awnings above that were stamped 'Le Champs'. The wind caused the smallest one to flap wildly. He turned at the corner, then made a U turn to drive in front.

The light was red at the intersection. He pressed on the brake and came to a stop. As he did, two men stepped out of the building. Both were foreign. The short man's few strands of hair blew vigorously out of place and he brushed them back with his fingers. His glasses had old-fashioned wire frames. He held his hand against his tie to keep it from blowing.

The other man was tanned across his face. His smooth colour made the rich blue suit he wore darker. He motioned and suddenly the car behind Ben honked. In the picture framed by the rearview mirror, Ben saw the wide chrome grill. The chauffeur had his arm outside the rolled down window. He honked again, pulling up as much as he could. As soon as the light changed, Ben drove off. He could see the two men getting into the Rolls. That's Julian Alexander he thought. He understood what Abe had implied by the tone of his voice.

Well, well. Wouldn't it be an opportunity to work for real money? Coming from Iran, it might be more than he could imagine. Wealth was stamped on Julian's face like a monogram.

Ben pressed on the gas, turned right on Wilshire, passed Veteran's Park and headed home to tell Alice about the interview. He had a lot to say. He whistled, thinking of money. He glanced at a demonstration in front of the Federal Building, then continued in the sun to Third Street. At their building, he parked in the garage and rode the elevator to the first floor.

When he walked into the apartment he saw Alice sitting on the green carpet, playing with Jules. Jules was standing, trying to walk. His whole face was determined, his cheeks red, the lips curled, his voice a squeal. Ben stood a moment, watching. Thank God I may have found a job, he thought. One I like.

'What are you doing, huh?' Alice asked. 'Do you want to stand up?'

Jules wobbled, holding on to her fingers.

She turned and saw Ben.

'I want you to drive with me to Westwood,' he said. He didn't sit down because he was in a hurry for them to go.

'Mr Freeman just called,' she said. 'He has to go to Switzerland and will call you back when he returns. It could be six weeks he said.'

Ben sat down. 'What else did he say?' he asked.

'He was very nice.' She picked up the pacifier and wiped it on her skirt. It was a Valentino skirt that hung past her knees. 'He said he definitely wanted to meet with you.' She shook the pacifier to make Jules suck. Then she sat down on the sofa beside Ben.

He noticed her perfume, her gold earrings. She had been waiting for him.

'Mr Goldstein called, too,' she said. 'He told me to tell you that Mr Alexander agreed to the salary. He wants you to call him back between eight and ten tonight.' Her voice showed that she was excited. 'Are you going to take it?' she asked. 'He sounded like you were.'

He nodded, not worrying, just as she wasn't. He relaxed, leaning back against the sofa cushion. 'Do you remember the café I saw opening and said I wanted to take you to? Well it isn't open, and that's one of the bakeries. Come on,' he said. 'Let's drive by. I'll tell you about it.'

3

'Ben,' Abe said, 'did I wake you?'

'No,' He stifled a yawn, one eye on the kitchen clock. It was five a.m. With one hand he began to retie the string to his pyjama bottoms.

'I wanted to catch you before you left for the mall. I need you to go by Westwood first. The bakers are expecting to work all day, but they can't because electricians are going to be rewiring. Lars should be there in a few minutes. Tell Scott and Carey to bake croissants. Ramon and Jose will be there. And tell them all to quit by noon. I'll be back by then.'

'What else should I tell them?' Ben asked.

'Introduce yourself,' Abe said. 'I've got to go now.'

Wilshire was already busy at six o'clock. He stopped at the Third Street light, then looked at his watch again. Everyone up and going to work waited in the early traffic. Polly's Pie Shop, ahead on his left, was closed. So was the blue First Interstate Bank. But the entrance to Zucky's was as crowded as the street, and he rolled down the window, the air cool, the light fog not burned off. He pressed lightly on the accelerator as the signal changed. The street was just wet enough for the tyres to hum. He drove past Lincoln Park, the deep grass coloured with birds feeding in the flower beds.

As he passed, the birds fluttered, then settled in the trees edging the sidewalk. He felt uneasy, and he wondered if he had been right in accepting the job. After all, he wouldn't have run a bakery at home. He could hide, doing it in L.A. But wasn't

L.A. supposed to be Hollywood when it came to working? Didn't everyone really want to act, direct, produce, or write? Did he? He pressed on the gas, watching the numbered streets pass. Ninth, Tenth, Eleventh . . . He thought that he probably shouldn't have taken it. Not that he wasn't going to work, or that he wouldn't try his best. He simply wondered ahead of time whether or not he should have. Whoever knew, and something had to, wasn't giving him a hint. Do what you will, it echoed back. And he looked out at the cars all on their knees at lights as far as he could see, and the sun bright around them. The light was truth, and the palms, the sounds of the tyres on the asphalt. But where was it in his life? What had led him to where he was? Shut up, he thought. Give yourself a chance. You might love it.

He felt wonderful for a moment. The sky was reflected in the glass store fronts, the highrises, the car windows. Everything he saw had an impulse that had begun it: he saw the cars move, birds fly past, a crane raising steel beams so high that he thought of the cable. He felt the same impulse within himself. He was glad to be up and out of bed, Le Champs before him now. He drove into Gayley Street, keeping in the left lane. He turned quickly at the stop sign and parked the Toyota in the yellow loading zone that Abe had told him about.

The stores along the block had shiny glass fronts that were all shut until nine. He walked toward the glass entrance of Le Champs, and saw the bakers. They wore white uniforms and sipped coffee at a table by the window.

He opened the glass door, hesitated, then pulled out a chair and joined them. Its wrought iron legs scraped against the tile floor. Lars was the oldest. Scott Massey and Carey sat across from him. Ramon, the head bread man, looked ill at ease. His black hair shone, and his clean white pants were potlike at his waist. Another Mexican sat next to Ramon. Jose didn't speak English. His dark hair was flecked with grey, his face brick red. 'That Jose can bake,' Abe had told Ben. Ben glanced at him. Jose looked as if he had been born in an oven, and without understanding a word of English, could have gotten up from the table, gone into the kitchen and baked anything.

'Do you know each other yet?' Ben asked. He relaxed when he saw that they didn't. 'Let me begin,' he said, 'by introducing myself.' He felt more at ease afterward. 'I'd like to know,' he said, and meant it, 'what you like to cook.'

When Abe came at noon, the bakers had gone. He brought a mouthful of notes with him. 'Ben, make a note,' he said, 'the clock is six minutes slow.' He looked about the room as Ben wrote it down. *Clock broken.* 'Why isn't it working?' Ben asked. Abe continued, 'Here's a number in Tustin of a man who sold us the oven. If the inspector won't pass it, tell him. It's Fletcher. F-l-e-t-c-h-e-r. He'll fix it if he wants to be paid – okay? Tell him I said so. Come on, let's go in the kitchen. I have a number of things for you to write down. Remember, the cappucino machine needs repair. One of the handles is broken.' Ben tried the loose handle then followed him into the kitchen. Abe picked up a five-gallon plastic container from the floor. He set it on a butcher top table. His belly swung as he prised off the lid with a spatula.

Leaning over, Ben could see the chocolate inside darker than pudding.

Abe dipped in his finger, then licked it clean. 'Here, Ben, try some.' He wiped chocolate from his lips with his hand.

Ben hesitated, then pushed his finger down to his knuckle into the icing. He brought it to his tongue. Anyone would have said ummm.

'Good, isn't it? Order another one from Westcott. And do you see that sink? Later on when Fasi comes (that's who Freddy hired to rebuild the kitchen) tell him the inspector says that it has to be a double sink. Have you met Freddy yet?' Abe washed off his hands in the basin.

'Huh uh. How do you spell Fasi?' Why, he wondered, did it have to be a double sink?

'Freddy is Julian's boy. The less you have to do with him the better. You can get Fasi's number from him.' Abe lifted another large canister, dried his hands on a cup towel, then opened the jar. The filling was mimeograph blue. He licked it from his fingers and dipped again. 'I like the blueberry better,' he said. 'Try some if you want, Ben.'

Ben finished another bite of chocolate, then watched his finger disappear into the purple gel.

'Good, isn't it?' Abe asked. 'Come in here, Ben. I'll show you something about Freddy. He decided to add shelves and paint the bathroom. So it would be bright. He chose orange. See?' Both of them stood in the doorway, then Abe flushed the toilet. It ran noisily as he looked about the room. 'Because he changed it at all, the building inspector said we had to add facilities for the handicapped. Customers can't even use the toilet, but we had to spend $5,000 more to equip it for hand-icapped people we'll never hire. Make sure to ask the building inspector about it. It will make him easier on us now.' He walked back into the kitchen, then the hallway. 'Over here, too. The refrigerator floor needs repair before the inspector comes. Fasi can do that.' He stood without speaking a moment. 'Can you think of anything else? Do you have questions? If not, let's go to Valley Mall. Are you doing okay?'

'Sure,' Ben said. 'And I'm supposed to get these things fixed, right?'

'Fix whatever needs it,' Abe said, holding the door open.

The traffic had multiplied; the air conditioner blew loudly as Abe started the ignition. Ben sat across from the driver's side and watched Abe ease into the lane. Abe turned left on Sepulveda. 'It's faster than the freeway now,' he said. He drove just as he talked, quickly. When he saw a chance to pass, he took it.

Ben looked at the notes he'd written on the narrow lined pad. Every time he had taken something down, he had starred or circled it, or made it larger or smaller than the point before so that he would remember what he had written. Now, everything looked the same, like graffiti.

He listened to Abe talk. He didn't want to interrupt. He would write everything down, get the store open. It didn't matter what it took. Abe wanted all his attention, and he would give it. Give him every minute, he thought, more than he asks for. Pay attention to each detail. Suspend yourself. Why? Somehow it was right; it was special. Maybe it was Abe.

Abe laughed, his voice throwing the bakery out the window. 'You'd like my wife,' he said. 'Lisa's friends are very cultured people, Ben. Like you. They go to the opera, the ballet, things I don't care for myself. Oh did she get mad when I was home.' His belly jiggled as he chuckled. 'One night this woman friend of hers asked me, "Abe how come you never go with us to the opera? I feel sorry for Lisa. Don't you care for music?" "Listen," I told her, "I love music. I love it more than you do. But we're born with certain things and others we have to get for ourselves. You need music and culture. Me, I don't. I was born cultured, but I didn't get enough sex. That's what I need – more sex!" Boy, did she blow up.' He stopped at a light, still laughing. He rubbed his palm against the steering wheel. 'I'm uncouth,' Ben.'

'Oh, you're not,' Ben said.

'Look at them,' Abe said. He pointed in the distance to cars in the Valley Mall parking lot. 'Look at all those customers.' He had to drive past three aisles to locate a parking place. He parked close to the mall entrance.

'Elaine,' Abe said as he shut off the engine and got out of the car, 'is going to be your right arm, Ben. I hired her from the hotel where Brenda and I are staying. She waited on tables in the dining room when we ate breakfast; she was there at dinner at eight. At eleven she was serving drinks in the bar. So I began to talk to her. "Don't you ever leave here?" I asked "What else do I have to do with my time?" she said. So I offered her a job.'

He followed Abe into the shopping centre, up the escalator

and along the aisle to Le Champs. At Le Champs, Ben stood a few feet back from Abe who introduced him. Elaine chewed gum but she was pretty. Her dyed black hair made her younger. She wore a white blouse over her big breasts, and pierced gold earrings. 'Hi,' she said. 'We've got an emergency, Abe!'

'What's wrong?' Abe asked, surprised.

'There's something wrong with the oven,' Elaine said. 'I called an electrician, Abe. Hi Ben.' Elaine sighed. 'You'd better talk to Rudy, too. He's having problems with the dough.'

'I bet Rudy is pushing the timers out of order,' Abe said. 'I talked to New Haven this morning. Let me give you the man's number, Ben, just in case.' He leaned over the oven front. 'It's area code 406.'

Ben took the pad out of his hip pocket.

'342-5156. Now come over here, Ben. I want to show you something else.' Abe pressed the off button, then pulled a lever high. 'Watch closely.' He set the timer for five minutes, turned the temperature to the degrees and pressed 'automatic'. 'I think it will be okay now,' he said. 'You got that? Now come with me, Ben.'

Past the wire-protected storage bin, the stainless steel mixer contained a tub of dough. The dough was marbled with dark streaks from Rudy's dirty hands. He dug it out of the tub by the handful. Behind it, loaves of bread lay on racks, cooling. Most of them were burned. Rudy sweated as he worked. He threw a heavy batch into the plastic trash bag.

'It couldn't be the flour, but he thinks it is.' Abe shook his head. 'Go ahead Rudy, try one more bake as soon as the oven is ready. Ben and I will get new yeast.'

The kitchen floor was covered with flour. Ben was careful as he walked across it. His soles made white tracks on the red tiles when he reached the front.

'I saw a health food place on Vine,' Abe said. 'It'll have the yeast we need. You ready? You know where Vine is?'

When they got in the car, Ben opened the glove compartment and saw an L.A. map with the rental papers.

'I don't use a map,' Abe said. He rolled down the window, turned on the air conditioning and blew out a big breath. 'Whew. Let's relax a minute, Ben. I won't take the freeway. Are you catching on how things run?' He braked, then shifted gears. 'It'll be easy for you.'

'It looks hectic to me,' Ben said. 'You know what you're doing.'

'That's the fun part – the first. In a month you won't have anything to do. You'll just sit back and tell everybody else what to do if you're smart.' He pressed on the gas, then slowed behind a car turning. 'Look at that, Ben. Are all the girls in California like that?' The blonde held up her thumb and had her small blouse tied rather than buttoned at the waist.

'You know,' Abe continued, 'you either work for someone or they work for you. I'm my own boss, Ben. I've lost more money than most people make, but it doesn't worry me. There's always more where that came from.' He took a cigarette from his pocket and offered one to Ben. He pressed in the lighter, then used it.

'My first year in the franchise business, I made over one hundred thousand and one forty the next. I was lucky and I learned why later. Do you know what a franchise really is?' He glanced across the seat at Ben. His voice deepened. 'You're selling hope to someone who is too scared to do it on their own. So you do it for them.'

Ben rolled down his window, the air blowing against his face. 'You make it sound easy,' he said. 'If it were, everyone would do it. There wouldn't be any franchises. You've proved you can already.' Then he saw Abe glow, like the tip of the cigarette. Yet he had meant it.

'You know what the hardest thing in business is?' Abe asked.

Abe didn't want an answer.

'The first time you start out. I was scared shitless the day I went into my own business.' Abe leaned back against the seat, driving with one hand. 'I like you Ben,' he said, 'I can talk to you. I wouldn't tell everyone that.'

He noticed Abe's gold watch and the careful way his hair was combed. The car too was washed and swept. Even his shirt, pooched out at his stomach, was starched and pressed.

'What did Julian say when you hired me?' Ben asked.

'About what?'

'My managing the bakeries?'

'I didn't ask him.' Abe frowned, then spoke louder. 'Don't bother with him, Ben. If you have a question, ask me. If I'm not there, then do what you think is best. Don't trouble Julian. Act just as if *you* own the stores.' He drove a minute without talking. The low buildings were all smog coloured, about to cough. Toward Hollywood, the streets narrowed and the traffic increased. 'Look at that!' Abe honked, then passed the Chevrolet in front. 'Avoid Nuri,' he said. 'He's Julian's accountant. I don't like him. He'll probably call you. He wants you to do bookkeeping. Don't.' He braked suddenly, and turned, the tyres screeching. 'There it is,' he said. 'I thought I could find it.' He parked and adjusted the rearview mirror, then switched off the ignition. 'Julian wants to look successful to his friends,' he said. 'He'll come in and taste the bread. Play along with him. He's just waiting to go back to Iran. These stores are toys.'

'He's rich?'

'He's rich,' Abe said. 'I don't know how rich. But he's told me some things about his work there. In Iran his income was five million a year, tax free.'

Ben waited for Abe to tell him more.

'If you have any questions for me, now is a good time for them,' Abe said. 'You're in charge when I leave.'

'You go tonight at ten?'

'And I'm coming back Thursday, unless you decide we

should open earlier. Julian will tell you. Don't worry. Just call every morning. I'll make any decisions you can't.'

'I think I'll go to work when Ramon does tomorrow morning,' Ben said. 'I'd like to learn how to bake.'

Abe nodded, his face pleased as he listened. 'All right,' he said. 'I can understand that. I did the same thing.'

At seven p.m. Ben got in his car, stretched, then started the ignition. He looked ahead of him, the traffic like a sculpture. It shone from start to finish, and he drove toward the freeway entrance. His first day at the bakery was over.

At I-10 and Eighth he exited, going forty miles an hour. He continued along Lincoln to Wilshire. He slowed to twenty. He drove past Freeman's dark glass highrise, then a number of other glass buildings.

He could see inside the offices even from the street, the panelling, the tall lampshades, the highest shelves lined with books.

Come to think of it, he didn't have business men for friends. He had writers or teachers or people he had met accidentally. None of them ran businesses. Business men didn't go where he did. Would Abe be at the library or in the next booth at a fast food place where he wrote? Or at a school? Abe wouldn't be in Hollywood either. During the day, didn't they stay in their offices? What did they do? What did they think about?

What do you think about? he asked himself. And he wondered what it would be like to be at home, in his bedroom, with the walls twice as high, the glass twice as thick and the panelling shining. Drawers of underwear and socks, neat stacks of laundered shirts, telephones in several corners of the room. In one drawer would be a cheque-book, with enough money to pay for whatever he wanted. If you're rich, he thought, what are you thinking about in that room?

That's how you make money. You think about it.

Julian had bought these stores, and a car place, a boutique,

33

apartments in Palm Springs, a suntan store. Freeman was going to Europe on business.

Talk to them, he thought. You have to. Because you want money too. He drove slowly, watching the traffic, glancing at the storefront displays.

The next morning although he arrived by five-thirty, Ramon and Jose already had worked several hours. The kitchen smelled of bread made with lots of yeast. The bright orange oven had a row of pulleys along the front. One opened a vent for air; another sprayed mists of water on to the loaves to make the tops more crisp.

Ramon was noisily setting a stack of trays into the humidifier. While Ben watched, Ramon closed the doors to the tall machine and stood on tiptoe to turn the dial. Inside, the machine was like a steam bath. The loaves sweated and puffed so that when they came out, ready to bake, they quivered. The humidifier made the separation of the layers distinct.

Back in the kitchen, every table was being used. By six Scott and Carey laid out sugary dough yellow with sweetmore. Scott flattened the dough evenly until it was consistent. Then he took a circular utensil and cut the dough into triangular pieces. He stood on one side of the white table and Carey on the other. Each began to roll triangles, mincing the widest corners flat so that the narrow points lay on top. Then Scott brushed the croissants with melted butter and put them into the humidifier.

Behind them, Jose stood at the cutting machine that turned out shapes of bread: baguettes, petit pain, boules. The loaves wiggled from behind a rubber roller and were placed on greased, floured trays.

The baking dough made the kitchen a place like nowhere else. Trays of breads, croissants, and cakes were put into and taken out of the ovens with a long wooden pallet. Scott and Jose sweated, tired, their arms taut. Their eyes even showed how tired they got.

Was the product ready? One taste, what was there to choose? Double fudge cakes, pale green princess cakes, cream puffs, dark mousses, strawberry cake, Bavarian cream cake, and croissants made plain or with chocolate, apricot, blueberry, cheese, and ham. The cash register had a bell and was new. Ben walked from the kitchen, wanting to applaud. Up front, sunlight hit against the glass shelves. It was eleven-thirty. He sat at a wrought iron table, and looked over his notes.

When he glanced up, he saw the polished green Rolls pulling into the loading zone. Surely that's not Julian already, Ben thought. A chauffeur opened the door, and Ben saw into the silver interior. He would have looked, regardless.

He saw Rose for the first time. She wore red slacks and a cotton blouse. Her turquoise and gold necklace hung to her belt, and she was talking. The balding man short enough for any one to pat on the head got out next. He leaned back in, speaking to Julian. Then came a man wearing a plaid suit with very wide lapels. His collar unbuttoned, he stood with his hands almost hidden on his hips. Julian got out last. He wore a European suit, a light blue ascot, and a gold ring that caught the sunlight. They stood like a flock of birds outside, then entered the bakery.

My, my, Ben thought.

'Ahhh,' Julian said, pointing them to a table. The gold in his front tooth matched his ring. He raised his chin, walking toward Ben. 'Good morning,' he said.

'Please,' Ben said, gesturing to the table. They have brought a music with them, he thought. 'I'm Ben Escobio,' he said.

'Certainly,' Julian said and nodded, his tongue quickly wetting his lips. He spoke up close to Ben's face. 'If there is any bread for today?' he asked.

'I'll get some,' Ben said. It's their voices, he thought. Melodic. Persian began to flow like water into the small bakery.

Julian sat down next to the window. Ben walked away from the table, seeing their reflections in the mirror. He's full of money already, Ben thought. He isn't hungry. The bakery suddenly was like a bank. They sat, Rose knowing how to make them laugh, her long gold earrings shaking. They must have cost a fortune.

Ben hurried through the hallway into the kitchen and saw Jose but not Ramon. The toilet door was closed. He could hear Ramon inside. 'We need the best loaf of bread you baked.' He nodded vigorously at Jose. Yes, he meant, you hear me. You understand me. The only word of English Jose had bothered to learn, was *no*. 'Where is a good loaf?' he asked.

Jose raised his shoulders, his eyes widening. 'No Englishe,' he said.

'Bread,' he said, louder. He looked around the room, loaves stacked on the butcher tables near by. 'Es okay?' he asked. The loaf felt heavy. Abe had told him to keep Julian out of the kitchen while the bakers perfected his recipes. Hurry, he thought. He didn't know if any of the bake-offs had been completely successful yet. All the bread looked good.

Jose shook his head.

'No?'

Jose shook his head again, exactly the same.

'Yes?'

Jose hesitated, then began. The Spanish, Ben thought, was much more frustrating than the Persian. He thought he caught words, confused and changed, and he listened. It was like chasing a cat. Finally, he broke in. 'Jose,' he said, 'Por favor, I need a bueno loaf of breado, OK?' He held one up for example. 'Donday?'

'No,' Jose said. He held up a loaf from another table, then handed it to Ben. '*Es bueno. Si.*'

'*Merci*,' Ben said quickly. He hesitated, trying to think. What was the Spanish for thanks? He set the loaf on a white plate. He dusted the crust with his fingers, got a knife from the drawer, then hurried to the front.

36

Sunlight crossed the small table and caught Rose's hair. 'Oh thank you, Ben,' she said. 'Julian cares so much about the bread.' Her English accent was exact. 'I've heard a lot about you,' she said.

He set the plate on the table, saw the canister of white napkins, the cups of coffee they had poured themselves.

'Should I cut it?' he asked.

'No. No.' Julian squeezed the loaf, then broke off an end with his fingers. Golden pieces of crust scattered across the plate. He began to chew. Everyone hushed, as if Julian had raised his hands, to speak. Ben was close enough to hear Julian chew. He looked at the orange gold pieces of Rose's necklace. At least eighteen carat. Julian waited, his jaw moving, then he swallowed. His voice was high. 'A little crisp,' he said. 'Hmmm?'

'Perhaps the vent was open too wide,' Ben said, surprising himself.

'Rose?' Julian raised his eyebrows.

She tried a smaller piece, but the short man refused. Their fat guest ate a large piece quickly, then slowly nodded toward Julian.

'Julian and I used to prefer the bread at a bakery in Paris,' she said. 'Do you know Paris?'

Ben caught her large eyes, the lashes like a doll's. 'No,' he said.

'Perhaps,' Julian said. 'We should open tomorrow?' He glanced at Mr Nuri who nodded without anyone but Ben and Julian seeing it. 'Yes.' Julian said to Ben. 'Can we?'

'Certainly,' Ben said. 'In the morning? I'll call Abe.'

'Or afternoon. It is for you.' Julian's whole front tooth was gold, and he sat back, a finger resting on it. 'We will depend upon it,' he said. 'Agreed?'

'Tell Brenda to call the girls,' Abe said. 'I won't be there; I have to be in Florida, Ben. Let me give you the number. Got a pen? Get in touch with the bakers. For a few days have everyone come. Try them all first. I'll be there soon. All right?'

'What time tomorrow?' Ben asked.

'Pick a time to open,' Abe said. 'Close when the customers leave. You won't have any trouble.'

4

Elaine's scream was like a big pot falling off a wall in the kitchen. He looked up, relieved to be far from her. She had perfected loudness; when he was around her, he had no defence. All she had to do to make him feel silly was answer a question in a voice ten times louder than his.

'Ben!' she called.

He walked into the kitchen dutifully about to criticize everyone. The display cases were lawns of peacocks and the straw bins, fields of manna. From the register, a customer could see inside the plentiful oven. It was time to open.

'Ben! Come here!'

Ramon held his arms behind his back, but his cheeks were red. Elaine laughed, her breasts shaking. 'Show him, Ramon'

Ramon brought the dough in front of him and held it at his chest.

'Ha ha ha ha ha ha!' Elaine ducked her head, her hands over her eyes.

The foot-long penis had big testicles and was sickly white.

'It iss for Elaine. She can take it home.'

'Put it in the oven,' Elaine said. 'I want to show it to Abe when he comes.'

'Or throw it away,' Ben said.

'Don't throw it away! It's mine!'

'I can make one in a minute,' Ramon said. 'Want me to show you?'

Then he got curious, even if it looked like part of Frankenstein. 'Yes,' he said. He watched Ramon's fingers shape lumps of dough. Half a minute, two twists, patting the balls, and Ramon had another. It looked easy.

Ben looked across at Lars who worked at a marble-topped table close to the hanging spatulas and long-handled spoons. He cracked two eggs at a time and dropped egg whites into a bowl, carefully.

'Are the girls ready?' Ben asked. 'I'm going to open the door.'

'Yes-ss! We've been waiting for you. I've trained them on the register. And they're supposed to know the French names.'

He used the brass key to turn the lock, then changed the sign to read 'Open.' A surprised girl outside passing by the corner, stopped. In a minute, several people were looking in. Ben watched, then waved, motioning them inside. 'Give everyone a taste of a croissant,' he said. That was it, give. Give them everything they wanted, atmosphere, delicious looking pastries, counter girls in beige pinafores. Give them French music, a smile, cleanliness. Give them friendliness, an ear, a French café. Loveliness, that kind of give. But charge them for it. An arm and a leg to begin, then more. See how much they would pay. Isn't that why people told others to 'smile', he thought? To see what they coúld get? Everyone smile, he thought.

He watched the customers until they had chosen what they would eat. The movie across the street let out, and the bakery was almost carried off. Bill baked another dozen trays of croissants. The counter girls began to perspire, and Ben turned on the air conditioning.

Rose came mid-afternoon. 'Hello!' she said. Her friends were on her arms, her hair, her small feet. 'Ben,' she said. 'It looks beautiful . . .' She picked out a piece of cake she wanted to try. 'I'll pay for it,' she said.

'No. You can't.'

'But I want to. Maybe you won't have enough of this one to sell. Let me pay.'

'It's your store.'

'Thank you,' she said, giving in.

Ben went back and checked the register tapes. $1,450 by four o'clock. Excellent. He could tell Abe, proud of what he had done. And Abe could take the same figure and proud of himself, tell Julian. Since Julian spoke Persian, it didn't matter who he told. The credit could be stolen intact.

He took a paper cup, added ice and pressed the rim of the cup against the lever that dispensed Tab. The drink foamed above the ice, and he filled it half-way. Customers waited to sit at the six small tables. When one cleared, he saw Rose put her purse on it. She waved at two friends outside who came in to join them.

'Elaine,' Ben said. 'What else do we need?' He counted the tray of croissants.

'Plain ones,' she said. 'Tell Scott to make a dozen ham if he has it.'

'Are the girls OK?'

'*Yes*. Would you tell Scott?'

When he came out of the kitchen, he saw Julian just sitting down at a free table close to the door. Mr Nuri and another man sat with him. Ben looked across at Rose who without calling, tried to get Julian's attention. After a minute, she quit.

Ben stood in the hallway. Inside his head was a floor-plan of the bakery. It included the handle of the refrigerator and the number of the repair man who still hadn't added caulking. Most of the numbers that Abe had given him had become commonplace. He could have turned anyone's head or taken their breath away, if they were impressed with knowing what should be done, by whom, and when. His eyes couldn't focus inside the bakery without the blueprint part of what he saw. What someone should be doing, or how something should be, had become instinct. He was like the watchdog who barked at anything suspicious.

Don't these croissants look good, he thought. In front of him stood a rack of trays with thirty croissants each. He took one with his fingers, bit, then tossed it into a waste basket. The moment it was out of his hand he wanted another. He agreed, choosing a larger one, which tasted as good. Behind the counter any of them could have as many as they wanted. They were as available as the air was outside. But on the other side of the counter, customers pawed the floor, waiting in line.

Wasn't that Julian's fat friend in the same wide lapel jacket? Yes. He and two friends sat beside Julian's table. That made Rose and her friends at one, two, three, and Julian at one, his friend next, and only one table for customers. Well, tell them, he thought. You're all taking up the place. How can we sell food if no one has a place to sit?

'Ben,' Elaine said. She was putting on lipstick without looking in the mirror. 'Have you seen all the Iranians? I hope we don't get bombed.'

'It's a party for them,' he said.

'I don't care what it is, do you realize anyone could drive by and toss a bomb through the window? I know a lot of people who would like to.'

'No one can sit down,' he said.

'That's what I'm telling you. Look, I think Nuri wants you.'

His eyes turned half an inch. Nuri motioned with his index finger. It curled, making little circles at him.

Despite himself, he wished for Abe.

'Mr Ben,' Nuri said into his ear. He leaned down because he stood and Nuri, who was so short, sat. Nuri blew smoke in his ear. 'Could you be so kind to bring us the sales? For today?'

'Now, Mr Nuri?' he asked.

'It is nothing, but if you would help, Julian and I would thank you.'

'Of course.'

He walked to the register, punched 6, then 1, 1, 1. The tape spun out, the figures exact. Over $1,900. Excellent. He took the tape to Nuri. 'Here,' he said smiling. 'The total tonight will be higher.'

'It is done. Excuse me, Ben. I thank you. It is nothing.'

He walked back to the counter. Nuri, he thought, had a certain authority that came from his attitude. Not like a policeman. More as a prosecuting attorney who was watching the crime. Their eyes met for an instant. Well, Nuri's glance meant, have you organized the inventory yet, how about the humidifier? Why won't it pass inspection; it's new? Everything that he hadn't done, made him want to faint.

Outside, a green Alfa Romeo u-turned at Gayley, then caught everyone's eye. It backfired, stopping in a No Parking area at Le Champs Westwood. Freddy got out, wearing bluejeans and a tee shirt that hung at his shoulders. He motioned to a couple at the corner of Gayley and Poole. Gold chains hung at his neck and on his wrist. The man had dark bushy hair, a big nose, and was smaller than the girl.

Ben sipped more coke.

The glass front reflected them talking. It soaked up the lights outside and brought them dazzling into the lighted bakery.

Freddy gestured more than he spoke. The girl had long hair that seemed to give her careful posture. Her shiny top followed the curve of her breasts and matched her bright pink mouth. Neither she nor the boy she was with laughed when Freddy did.

Abe had told him that Freddy once had bet him ten dollars he could get a date with any girl he saw. 'OK, that one,' Abe had pointed out a girl who had just entered the car place. Freddy hurried across to her and began to talk. 'Do you like to date rich guys? Millionaires? Well, I'm rich. Will you go on a date with me?' She had left with him a few minutes later.

But this girl wasn't impressed. Her lips moved but her mouth didn't soften. She brushed her arm under her thick hair and stepped away from the curb. Then she and the boy with her waited in front of the window while Freddy entered the bakery hurriedly. He nodded at Julian, and stopped at Rose's table a second. He continued past to Ben.

'Ben,' he said and put his arm around him so that the gold bracelet touched against Ben's neck. Up close Freddy smelled of after shave and his arm felt light. 'Ben, how are you?' he asked. 'Can I do something for you?'

'What?' Ben asked. 'Is it something I wish you wouldn't?'

'Seriously, I have a favour to ask.'

'What favour, Freddy?' Ben leaned forward to get out from under Freddy's arm. 'Have you asked Julian?'

'I promised that girl outside you'd hire her and her boyfriend. Do it for me, will you?'

'Why did you tell them that?'

'Let me bring them in. Please. Talk to them? Look at her, Ben. Don't you think she's pretty? Please talk to her.'

When she came into the bakery, her large breasts and slim waist were accentuated by her walk. 'Hello,' she said, her English accented.

Ben took his mind off everything else. 'Have you worked in a bakery before?' he asked.

She didn't bat an eye.

'Yes,' the guy said. His accent was French, too.

'Where are you from?'

'Paris. Freddy, he says that you have a job for us? No?'

'What kind of work are you looking for?'

'Here. At the bakery. We can do anything you like.'

'The pay is minimum wage. We're trying out people.'

'It's the same everywhere. That's OK.' He couldn't keep from looking at the food.

'Can you come early in the morning? You don't have to work the same hours, do you?'

'We need to work,' he said. 'We have no money. I can start now if you want.'

44

'Take some croissants with you. Come in at six in the morning. Tell me if they're good,' he said.

'They're too big,' she said. 'Much too big. They should be so.' She held up her hand then suddenly her large white teeth showed, as she smiled. 'It is so American,' she said.

'One for each of us?' the boy asked, pointing to the croissants.

'What's your name?'

'Maurice,' he said. 'Maurice Samyn.'

Ben looked at the girl. 'I am Madeleine,' she said. 'How many can we have?'

He watched them leave a few minutes later, both of them eating from the full sack of pastries.

At ten that evening Elaine and the girls took off their shoes and sat on the wooden stools, their stocking feet resting on the supporting bars. Rose and Julian now chatted at the same table, and the breads attracted even more Iranians. Laughter had broken out inevitably as albumen from a cracked egg. No one left his table, and customers lingered at the counter. Suddenly, nothing was hurried. As if the business had been open for years. Many customers didn't know that the store was new. Ben felt relieved and happy. He had done all right. He went into the kitchen where Pablo washed the trays in steaming water. Then he stepped past, into the bathroom, and shut the door. He saw his reflection in the mirror as he walked to the sink. He stopped a moment. Yes, you're here, he thought. In this bathroom. In this kitchen. He walked to the commode and listened to himself. But what am I doing here, in charge of it? Where is everyone I know? He looked at his watch. He wanted to go home.

The bakery was open.

5

March

'Ben, go ahead,' Abe said. 'You go first. You're doing beautifully. I got the month's receipts this morning.'

Ben took the spiral notebook from his shirt pocket and turned back the cover. 'I wish you were in L.A.,' he said. 'Are you ready?' The controls on the humidifier were higher up than Westwood ordinances allowed. Ramon had to stand on tiptoe to turn them on. The cappucino machine didn't boil water even if it looked like it cost a fortune. The double sink hadn't arrived. Mr Weeks, the electrical inspector, gave them one month to comply with his recommendations. 'But that's not the biggest problem, Abe,' Ben said. 'Nuri – '

'One minute. Let me give you a name,' Abe said. 'It's Samuel Schiff in New Rochelle. Ask him if the dials can be moved. The number is 212-711-0300.'

'If he says no, I call you back?'

'Explain it to him. He wants paid. Go ahead.'

'Nuri's not paying for anything, Abe. I've found bills *everywhere* and they go back for months. He hasn't paid a single one since I've been here.' He was surprised that Abe didn't answer at once. 'I put the bills in the register for him, but he leaves them. If I try to hand them to him, he won't take them.'

'Is there one addressed to me?' Abe asked. 'Check the returns for New York City.'

'I see it.'

'Would you mail it to me this afternoon please?'

'What about the rest?'

'You'll have to get Nuri to pay them. I'll call Julian now. Don't you meet with Nuri today?'

'Yes, and Julian says a relative will start work tomorrow. He wants her to cashier. Do we have to have more relatives?'

'That's Anya. Ignore her, Ben. Keep the girls on just as if she wasn't coming.'

'Could you do something about Freddy? The cooks don't want him in the kitchen any more. And he left a four hundred dollar I.O.U. in the register and took out cash last night.'

'What? One at a time. He what?'

He'd forgotten the cutter that needed a different plug to pass inspection. 'When are you coming?' he asked Abe.

'I wish it was today. It's eighteen degrees and snowing in Philadelphia.'

'Is Brenda there?'

'One minute,' Abe said. Brenda picked up a phone and her low voice was laughing. 'I've heard about your problems with Iranians,' she said. 'I understand.'

'See, Ben. We haven't forgotten you,' Abe said.

'Congratulations,' Brenda said. 'Abe says you did over $3,500 yesterday.'

He had already called the cash register repair and had learned how to put in the new tape and to program prices. He glanced across, at Maurice and Madeleine. Maurice was grinning.

'Ben, it's my other line. You want me to call you back?'

'This afternoon if you can.'

'I'll be in Washington. You can call me tonight at home.'

When Ben hung up, he had twenty minutes to make it to Nuri's office. He stood, adding items to his list. Call the city health inspector. Tell Elaine to order what Ramon wanted for the light pastries. Find out who had built the shelves that were about to fall any second in the storage room. And meet with Nuri. He closed the notebook and stuck it in his pocket.

'Ben?' Maurice asked. He wiped the long shiny counter with

a white cup towel. 'Can we take croissants home with us? Hey? Why do we throw them out?'

'Um hmmm.' He looked up. 'You can have everything that's left when we close. Abe says we can't sell them.' He glanced up at the clock.

People at the bakery said negative things about Mr Nuri. He was Julian's shadow but smaller, always in a suit, black pointed-toe shoes, an unpressed white shirt, a blue tie and glasses. 'That old man,' Abe had said, 'he's nothing.' He had puckered as if to spit out a taste on his tongue. 'He wants you to be responsible for money. *Don't be.*' 'Mr Nuri, Rose had said, and raised her eyebrows, 'he and Julian think they're still in Iran.' 'Who is he?' Scott had asked in the kitchen. 'Why is he always hanging around watching?'

'He's Julian's partner,' Ben had said. 'He's keeping an eye on us.'

'Get him out of here,' Ramon had said. 'We don't want him.'

He had known people like Nuri all his life; teachers who enforced rules made for students years before, salespeople who couldn't hide their delight to be out of an item you wanted, preachers who believed that they held a lottery ticket to heaven, friends who couldn't make a mistake in grammar. Nuri had the inflexible viewpoint that he knew best.

By the time Ben left the bakery it had begun to rain. He hurried, unlocked the car door, then got in, his jacket soaked, his slacks spotted. His hair was wet against his forehead. The windshield clouded over from his breath.

He wiped the glass with a kleenex so that he could see out. The wipers beat rhythmically. When the windshield cleared, he carefully pulled into the Westwood traffic.

At the car company, he parked in front, put a dime in the meter, and hurried through the lobby. He nodded to Patrick whose last name he didn't remember. Patrick was over forty, and managed car sales.

The door to Mr Nuri's office was open. As Ben entered, he saw him, behind the vinyl desk, a single unoccupied chair in front. Nuri smoked, the grey fumes winding toward the neon light overhead.

Ben hesitated.

'Come in, Mr Ben,' he called. 'Please.' He motioned for Ben to sit. He puffed, then laid his cigarette on the amber glass ashtray.

'Thank you.'

Nuri opened the right-hand drawer of the desk. As he did, ashes dropped from the cigarette in his mouth, on to the papers before him. He brushed them off quickly, the grey smearing. He pulled a file from the drawer, let it fall back, then took out a brown folder. 'It is the Westwood cheque-book,' he said. 'This is Wells Fargo Bank. Yes, let me see.' His fingers ran across the written in account name at the bottom, 'Valley Mall'.

'One minute, do not worry,' he continued. He leaned down and pulled on the drawer to his left. The drawer opened with difficulty. 'It is here, I am sure of it,' Nuri said. He lifted out a blue portfolio and laid it on the desk. He saw another Wells Fargo cheque-book and brought it out. 'I am ready,' he said, puffing on the cigarette, 'at last. What to do, but we should pay the expenses! Abe, he call Julian this morning. It is no problem, do not worry. Did you bring them? Go ahead. We will do it together. This minute.'

Oh? Ben was surprised. He opened the briefcase Alice had given him and took out the bills. He could see that Nuri planned to involve him in bookkeeping. Oh I know how to, he thought. He glanced at Nuri. No, I won't do it no matter what you think.

'I have the bills sorted,' Ben said. 'Here.' He held them up. He had found them in trash cans, behind the register, on shelves in the kitchen, in the bathroom. How many had been lost already? He handed the stack to Nuri. He pushed back his chair and started to get up. It's your mess, he thought.

'This one,' Mr Nuri said. 'One minute, please.' He pulled the first envelope from under the rubber band. He motioned for Ben to sit.

Ben scooted the chair back to the desk and looked at him.

'What is the bill for?' Nuri asked. His tone changed, and he waited. He handed Ben back the whole stack of bills.

Ben looked down at the invoice. 'For milk,' he said, nervous. He laid the stack on the desk between them.

'Ah. For the materials raw. It is so. And for what time?'

'I'm not supposed to do bookkeeping,' he said.

'No. It is simple. I show you later. Mr Ben, from what day to what day for milk?'

He scanned the statement, the information difficult to interpret. He felt Mr Nuri's eyes on him. 'It doesn't say. It would have to be about when the bakers started. This is their first bill. It's a computer form.'

'But for how many days?'

'I'd have to ask Ramon.'

'Good. It is done. We do not pay it now. What is the next one?'

Ben reached across and took another envelope from under the rubber band. He took a long minute to look at his watch. 'The electric bill. It's past due. For two months, for January and February. See?'

'Ahh, for the electricity. It is so.' Nuri reached out his hand for the statement, spread it flat against the desk, dropping ashes on to it, and hesitated. 'Four hundred eighty-two, is it?'

'Yes.' Ben sat back in his chair.

'Just a minute.' Nuri picked up the pen. He began to write in a florid script. Ben watched him, then looked away.

'It is done.' Nuri handed him the cheque.

Ben looked at it, then was surprised. He held up the cheque. 'Mr Nuri,' he said, his voice uneasy.

Nuri laid down his pen before he answered.

'"Conserve energy" is their slogan. The cheque should be made out to the Pacific Electric Company. The company just wants everyone to conserve energy.'

'Ahh.' Nuri blushed, quickly taking the cheque, tore it in

two, and marked through the record. He ran his fingers across the statement. 'Would you underline the company for me, please?'

'Of course.' So he can't read them, Ben thought. And he's in charge of paying bills.

'Each time, as we pay?'

'Certainly.' Could that hurt, to do little things? Circle company names? Point out dates? Ben took the next envelope. Something had changed on Mr Nuri's face. His fingers relaxed around the cigarette he smoked. He leaned one elbow against the desk. He looked relieved.

'I'll be glad to help,' Ben said.

'I work twenty-eight years for Julian,' Mr Nuri said. 'Every morning I am in my office by seven, Mr Ben. I work until six in the evening. Not one day do I miss.'

Ben barely nodded.

The voice deepened, the accent more accentuated. 'I sign every cheque for the company. No one else ever. Not Julian sign. No one.'

'How many were there?'

'All day, only I sign. We have millions of dollars every month. It is a lot of cheques.' He puffed, letting the smoke out. 'Mr Ben, every morning I go to work, it is the same. I say hello to everyone and on my desk is a flower. Without fail. I do not know who brings it. The employees, they find me gentle.'

Ben listened, interested.

'A woman she call yesterday. She is in trouble, in Belgium. "Oh Mr Nuri, I find you." She is crying. "Do not worry," I tell her. "Julian and I will help you get work." She has no husband. What can she do? She work for us twenty-five years.' He paused, smoking the cigarette.

'You should help her, Mr Nuri.'

'Yes.' His voice high. 'We must. But for Julian it is hard. I see him worry. He does not know what he will do. What he do here? Who will help him?' He waved his cigarette, increasing the smoke.

'Why did he start these businesses?'

'For the boy. For Freddy. And what he does? Nothing. He is with his girlfriend. He rides in his car. What he cares about?' Nuri puffed, shaking his head.

Ben could answer it. Freddy came into the stores for money in the register. Or, if he was hungry, for a croissant and coffee. On the way he would go into the kitchen and give orders. Nuri had sat every day at the bakery, his eyes observing. And Julian sat at home, Rose said, in his bathrobe and smoked. He talked a lot on the telephone.

It is everywhere, such unhappiness, Ben thought. In my life, in yours. Sometimes we do not know what to do. What can we do about it? It will go away. He looked at Nuri, at the watery eyes behind the clear glasses, the bald head and few strands of grey hair. I like you, Mr Nuri, he thought. Do you like me?

Ben picked up the next bill. 'Are you ready?' he asked. 'It's for flour.'

'Ahh. For the material raw.' He nodded quickly.

'It's high, Mr Nuri. For a one week period, it's eight hundred dollars. But part of that is inventory.' He saw that Nuri didn't understand. 'In storage,' he said. 'For the next few days. For tomorrow and the next day. Let me ask Ramon. You see, Abe picked the companies we order from and Ramon orders the amounts. I know nothing about it.'

'Yes, it is so. Do we pay?'

'Let's wait.' He took the next one.

'Julian and I,' Mr Nuri said, 'We thank you Mr Ben. Julian asked me to tell you for him. You do a lot, I know. I see everything. Freddy he yak yak yak. Rose she yak yak yak. Everybody is boss.'

Ben nodded, about to speak.

'Julian is president, Freddy is vice-president. You are manager. Anya, what will she be? Director?'

'And I have to listen to them.' Ben handed the next bill across the desk.

'I know.'

'There,' Ben said, his finger on the amount due.

'It is so.' Nuri opened the cheque-book then began to fill in one of the green cheques. He looked up before writing in the amount. He puffed on the cigarette and returned it to the ashtray. 'You see what I do,' he said. 'Wait a minute, it is easy. You can learn. I debit cash. Here.' He wrote in the figure $415. 'And I credit the electrical. I make it easy for anyone. For a child. You can do it.'

'I see.' He looked at all the figures, searching for a balance. All the entries were in Nuri's script. He saw the column. Three million six hundred thousand forty-two dollars and fourteen cents. One, two, three . . . seven figures. He glanced up.

Nuri put his finger over the balance. Ben pretended not to notice.

It would take hours to go through the bills so slowly. He was already late to Valley Mall. The past due telephone, he reminded himself. The gas. Find the important ones. 'This is for the telephone,' he said, circling the name on the bill.

'Ah. It is so.'

Ben took the cheque, then opened another envelope. He would have liked to have tossed it in the air and gotten down to brass tacks. You, Mr Nuri, he wanted to say, tell me everything. Is there three million in the account? Why so much? Isn't it one of many accounts? How much money does Julian have? That was what he wanted to know. He didn't give a hoot about the bills. Tell me about your money. Or the revolution, he thought, about you and your wife you mentioned. About Iran . . .

He wanted to reach up, knock on Nuri's forehead and have a little door open. If he looked through, he would see inside the nearest room, still burning with revolution, dark with intrigue about money in and out of the country. Abe had told him that Julian got a lot of money out for other people. A businessman in Iran would hand Julian a million dollars on a handshake and meet him three months later in Switzerland to pick it up. Julian would take nothing for doing it.

Oh Nuri wanted to go back. So did Julian. All the men did. Ben saw that. They congregated, buzzing, suddenly one then the other on top of what was said. At the first break in Khoumeni's power, they would hurry home the way they came. Like a rush of water.

'And have you always worked with Julian?' Ben asked. Then he thought: ask him what he wants to talk about. He's not going to give you any information about them.

Nuri's face reddened. 'What you ask, Mr Ben? If I always work with Julian? I am foreigner in Iran. For twenty-eight years I live there, I am from Iraq.' He laid down the pen, and lighted another cigarette. 'It is what you know Baghdad. You heard?'

'Of course.' But he was not sure exactly where it was other than in the Bible.

Nuri waved his hand in circles, and nodded. 'I was banker in my country until I was fifteen.' He raised his eyebrows. 'A revolution. I go to Turkey.' He shrugged.

'A revolution?'

'Poof. Another revolution. There have been many in my country.'

'But why did you leave?'

'My family. It was known in all villages.' He puffed. 'What I do? My father was in the government. I could not hide.'

'Did you take money out?'

'Nothing.' He waved his hand. 'Nothing! We lose a lot.' His voice rose; it was loud. 'Everything, Mr Ben.'

'Well, how much was it?'

He didn't know. He shrugged. 'Today, even more. Then, ten, twenty million.'

'You didn't get any of it back?' Maybe it would be hundreds of millions today, Ben thought.

'It does not matter. Poof, it is gone. What is it, a revolution?'

He's translating, Ben thought. Was he thinking in Persian or Iraqui? He could see the brightness in Nuri's eyes; Julian's money meant nothing. His own did, what did it matter if it was gone? Millions and millions and in Iraq, *he* was the owner. Oh go back and get it, he thought.

'It is the wind, Mr Ben. It comes.' He waved his fingers to the left and leaned left. 'Wait. There is nothing to do. It will turn back. Do not worry. It blows the other way.' He waved his fingers right and bent right. His fingers were dark, delicate. He moved as if he were dancing.

'But it's terrible, Mr Nuri. Everything is changed, isn't it?' Look who you really are, he thought.

Nuri's brows rose; he looked up, to the ceiling. 'It always changes back,' he said.

'You were very rich,' Ben said.

Nuri nodded, his face animated, the smoke rising past him. 'It is nothing,' he said.

'Mr Nuri,' Ben said. 'You'll be able to go back to Iran soon. Khoumeni will be overthrown. And Julian and all of you will be better off for it.'

Nuri's lips showed small yellow teeth and he puffed. 'Yes,' he said. 'I hope so, Mr Ben. But the business there . . . she is ruined.'

When Ben left, he was so late that he didn't bother to hurry. He stopped at the bottom of the stairs and washed his hands in the lavatory. Then he noticed a new automobile that Freddy had bought at auction. The 1969 Cadillac had fins with tail lights like wands. It was the colour of a Hallowe'en pumpkin. It had been cut out just behind the front seat and customed into a pick-up truck. On a starlit night in Teheran it would have been a jack-o'-lantern speeding along the highway.

Who would Freddy get to take it off his hands? A Chevrolet that cost five thousand dollars in the States would sell for twenty thousand in Iran. A used Chrysler Imperial costing eleven thousand here would retail at forty thousand there. When Freddy saw the prices of cars in L.A., he rejoiced. He could sell them for many times what he bought them for and impress Julian. He bought cars at auction, parked them in his driveway in Beverly Hills, and waited for them to sell. Few did. But on each one, he could have made three or four times in Teheran what he paid in L.A.

Ben hurried outside, crossed the street in the rain and got in his car. He drove first to Valley Mall and met with Elaine about computerizing the payroll, then to Le Champs Westwood.

Wasn't it wonderful, he thought, the diversity in life? It didn't come from anything he did. It was like the rainstorm he drove in. He understood Nuri a lot better. He stopped at a light, looked at the other drivers around him. They could be anyone on earth. And no matter what they were thinking, they pressed on the gas just as the light changed. Come into my life, he thought, looking at it all, and the colourful, wet stores streamed along as he speeded.

He parked in the loading zone and could see how crowded the bakery was, even in bad weather. From the car, the whole block seemed under the shade of a tree in a rainstorm. Yet inside, the lights were brilliant.

He covered his head with his raincoat and hurried across the sidewalk and into le Champs. Everywhere, customers were speaking French.

'Maurice,' he said. 'We are catching on with your friends, huh?'

'*Oui*.' Maurice poured coffee into a white filter. His hands shook, and a customer waited at the counter. 'Louise called,' he said. 'She cannot work tonight.'

'Ben,' Ramon said. He stood in the doorway to the kitchen. His hands were on the sides of his waist where the strings of his apron were tied. He motioned. 'Can I talk with you a minute?' He disappeared through the narrow hallway into the kitchen.

56

Maurice spoke slowly in French.

Ben walked through the hallway, into the kitchen. The floor was thick with flour, and pots and pans were stacked in the single sink. The cutter whirred, giving off a burning smell.

'Yes?' Ben said.

Ramon forced a smile. It was meant critically, as if he were laughing at something. 'You are manager and I'm not,' he said.

Ben waited for him to continue. He didn't think Ramon was smiling at that.

'If I were,' Ramon said, 'I'd change certain things.'

'I'm sure of it,' Ben said, smiling.

'Did you know that Maurice gave those croissants to his friends? None of them paid.'

For a moment, neither said anything. Blame hovered in the air, batting its wings, then landed on Ben's nose. It twitched, angrily. He was sure it was true. Ramon's lips quivered suddenly into a broader smile. Both of them saw it, like a flag.

What business is it of yours? Ben thought. But it was out. It was his responsibility.

'I'll take care of it,' Ben said. Then he went into the hallway and counted the number of cakes that Scott had baked. He saw Maurice, just outside, shining the oven. Maurice's eyes turned toward him. Maurice clearly was uncomfortable.

Ben walked up to him and looked inside the oven at the baking bread. 'Did you give croissants away?' he asked. 'No one paid?'

'You told me I could.'

'I what?'

'Tonight they will be thrown away,' Maurice said. 'I should give my friends old croissants?'

Ben was angry for a second. 'You shouldn't give them anything,' he said. He watched Madeleine standing, facing them both.

'For the profit, huh? The business is so important, Ben?'

'Yes, it is.'

'I am not like you,' Maurice said.

'Neither am I,' Madeleine said. Her lips swelled as she spoke. 'I would not be like you for anything.' She made her eyes wide, holding her brows up, staring.

'I wouldn't want you to be.' Ben watched her stare, his eyes feeling mad too, and he raised his brows up toward his forehead, mimicking hers.

'You are so ugly, Ben. You are so selfish.' She managed to raise her brows even higher than his.

'Thank you,' Ben said. 'Neither of you can give any more away.' He stared, his mouth twisted. He wanted to say boo.

'I don't thank you,' Madeleine said lowly. Then she raised her voice angrily. 'I hate you, Ben!' She looked away, untied the frilly apron and took it off. She let it drop on the floor, and hurried, walking on it, past the counter, through the tables still busy with her friends.

'I go too,' Maurice said. 'You sell the croissants. You watch the profit. You are boss.' He reached the door, just as Madeleine left.

Ben opened his mouth. He saw them going outside, the door closing, them crossing the street, Maurice hurrying to catch her. All at once, every eye in the bakery was on him. No one spoke. The croissants were still in their hands. No. Wait. What had happened? He turned, checking the coffee in the pot, the pastries in the bins. The clock. Act as if they are supposed to go.

Everyone began to talk, and another customer walked in. Ben stood at the counter, where he was.

He started to explain to the customer choosing a croissant. This isn't part of my job. I'm in charge. I don't work behind the counter.

The man's eyes told him to hurry.

Wait a second, Ben wanted to say. He said nothing but saw the Rolex watch, the tailored check raincoat across the man's arm.

'Do you have six apricot?' the man asked.

Smile. He rattled the thin sack opening it. 'Have you tried the cheese?' Ben asked. The door opened: several other customers walked in. They seemed to fill up the place, and he noticed Maurice's friends leaving. A friend of Madeleine's stared at him. Her face had an ugly expression. He hoped that she wouldn't say anything. The tables were dirty and needed cleaning. Go ahead. It's part of your job, he thought. *Everything is* really. Isn't it? 'Yes?' he asked the next customer. 'All our products are made from one hundred per cent natural ingredients. Have you tried a cheese croissant?' He held one up in tissue. Get him to buy two, he thought. Go on.

'Could I get a coffee?' the first man asked.

'Sure,' he said. 'It's free.' It wasn't, and there wasn't a cleaned place to sit.

'A cheese and a chocolate,' the customer said. 'Thank heavens, the rain has stopped.'

He could see that the lady already knew what she wanted. He picked them up with tissue and walked to the register to take her money.

He looked up, at the chalkboard menu. A dollar and forty cents didn't sound right for cheese. They should charge one seventy-five. Make a note, he thought.

'Can I hand you this?' The woman had a clear rain hat, and held a stack of dirty plates and coffee cups. Two of her friends waited at the table. 'Don't you have table service?' she asked.

He shook his head, dropped the plates in the sink, and went back to the line. 'Coffee's free while you're waiting,' he said. 'If you want to eat at a table, would you mind clearing one?' Well why not? He rang another seven dollars into the register. 'If you haven't tried them,' he said, 'you should get blueberry and a cheese.' He handed another to a customer, then a cheese. The cheese was grilled inside it, and had spread on to the top. It looked delicious. He took the money and the dishes the customers gave him. Then he got a wet cloth and wiped the counter. He stepped behind the noseguard, took another cheese and walked to the hallway. He bit into the croissant. It tasted sweet yet salty, rich on his tongue. He took another bite. He looked across at the thick blueberry. It looked better. You should be taking a cheque to Elaine, he thought. Call and explain. Instead, Ben hurried over, got a blueberry croissant and bit into it. The filling was delicious. He took another larger bite and began to dial. He saw another customer. The phone at Valley Mall Le Champs was busy.

The door opened. The movie across the street had let out, and customers waited in line outside even. The rain had stopped completely. On the street, people looked in, wondering why everyone was lined up. He rang three different purchases and looked at the bread which never sold. 'All the bread is one-half price,' he said.

'What are the long ones called? How much are they?'

He bagged one then two. 'The whole wheat is really delicious,' he said. 'Would you try some?' He cut the ends of a loaf and made small slices to taste.

'Is that the last apricot croissant?'

A minute later, the phone rang. He hurried to it, and answered on the fourth ring.

'Ben.' Alice's voice was excited.

'I'm kind of busy,' he said. 'And I'm going to be late.'

'Mr Freeman called. He wants you to call him when you get a chance. He's back from Switzerland.'

'All right,' he said. 'Can I call you?' Ben told her bye, then hurried to wait on the next customer.

Ten minutes later he took a mousse out of the showcase and ate it with a plastic spoon. The taste was disappointing. He finished the bite and tossed the empty plastic cup into the garbage. Ummm, he thought, looking at the thick cherry cake in the refrigerated display case. He opened the glass and cut a piece at the marked places. The first bite he took tasted like the mousse. I don't know if Julian can afford having me wait on tables, he thought. He took another bite. He threw the rest in the trash. He reached inside the refrigerator and took out the last piece of chocolate cheesecake.

You should be going home soon, he thought. He had called Elaine, but her girls lived too far away to help him. She was needed at Valley Mall. No one else had been able to work. She would keep trying to find someone for him. There were six more hours until eleven.

The time passed slowly.

At ten, he munched a plain croissant, making himself fuller. Just in front, he saw the Rolls grille pull up, then the car stop, and Julian get out first. Rose was next, Mr Nuri, then several of their friends Ben recognized. Oh no. He watched them come in.

Julian talked outside, his foot on the fire hydrant while Rose came in. She wore enough gold necklaces to start a boutique. She smiled, as no one else did. As if she had no pretensions.

'What would you like?' he asked, clearing the tables.

'You want me to do that?' she asked.

'No. No.'

She sat back. 'I don't want anything. I don't think Julian does. Are you working at the counter?'

'Maurice and Madeleine needed off,' he said. 'I don't mind.'

But he did.

He looked down at the floor and shook his head. Then he went to the back and found a broom in the bathroom. He would tell Ramon to always flush the commode. How could someone be a baker and not do it? Tell him to wash his hands, too, he thought. And clean up the store room. He walked back into the front, carrying the broom. He ignored Julian and Nuri and began to sweep.

He was sure they noticed him. He swept meticulously, yet fast. He took a wet rag and rubbed across the tile floor, over two spots he'd seen as long as the bakery had been open. They came right up. He swept near Julian's shoes, and he thought about how much those very soles had touched Iran. Go home, he wanted to say. If you hadn't been so greedy, you wouldn't have had to leave.

Mr Nuri grinned, his hands up, making a question.

'Will you do everything, Mr Ben?' he asked. 'The bills? The hiring? The inspections? The payroll? Now the sweeping?' He waved his hand. Why not?

Oh, Ben thought. I don't like this. There was nothing wrong with good honest sweeping. He could lick the floor with his tongue if he had to. But why? For money?

He stood up and walked behind the counter.

No.

Knock it off, he thought. You'd be making a fool of yourself if people could hear you.

He looked up, when the door opened.

Madeleine wore a fancy blue dress and her face was overdone. The flush on her cheeks made her look as if she had been running. Her smile made her look like a third-rate actress.

'Oh Ben,' she said.

Maurice walked up to the counter, his hands on the glass. Both of them had been drinking.

'Hello, Madeleine.'

'Should we come in the morning?' she asked. Her smile sweetened to a dimple.

'At six,' Ben said. 'You will not give the croissants away?'

'No,' she said. And she laughed. 'Ben,' she said, 'your face. You were so unhappy. I am sorry.'

Ben nodded, smelling her perfume. He could go home. He did not have to worry who would open the bakery in the morning. That was all he cared about.

6

April

More Iranians. Every day they were at Julian's car agency, fresh from Iran and waiting for news. The slightest tidbit could have been auctioned. Outside the brick building, their cars usually took up the metered parking places. Only the men came, mostly in shirt sleeves, their pants and shoes noticeably foreign. They met there, nervous as ants, their eyes larger than normal, their voices high.

'They've been meeting since eight o'clock,' Patrick said. He sat on the leather sofa in the showroom and read a magazine.

'Is Nuri in his office?'

'He's with them. It's just Julian, Nuri, and Freddy.' Patrick crossed his legs and laid down the magazine. The ashtray in front of him on the blond coffee table spilled over with crushed cigarette butts.

The phone on the nearest desk began to ring. Once, twice, three times. When Patrick picked up the receiver on the fourth ring, the caller had hung up.

There was nothing to do but wait. Ben looked at his watch, then around the showroom. He sat down, picked up a magazine, and said nothing. *Playboy*. Its pages rustled as he turned them.

Patrick raised his eyebrows, shook his head, and blew out smoke. He rolled his eyes. 'I probably don't have to tell you they're closing this place,' he said. He puffed, then exhaled. 'Well, Julian says he is. Freddy says he isn't. That's why they're meeting.'

'Who told you that?' Ben asked.

'They're going to close everything sooner or later. I've heard them, but I don't pay attention.' He tapped ashes into the ashtray. 'They don't know what they're doing, you know. It might be the best thing. I wanted to warn you.'

Ben flipped the pages to the *Playboy* centrefold. He pulled out the pin-up, and the girl's legs surprised him. No wonder they couldn't sell cars.

'When did they tell you?' he asked.

'Just now,' Patrick said. 'Don't be surprised if they tell you, too.'

Ben heard Julian's voice, then footsteps on the stairs. Their meeting had ended.

He hurried past Julian's broad smile, up the steps to Nuri's office. Mr Nuri, he would say, is it true? Are you closing the businesses? Ben would ask it politely. He enjoyed Nuri's good manners. They let him show his own. As if the manners were property, real, and the starting point of everything they said. I respect you, he meant by his. You and I can be polite. We can be honest.

He entered the office and sat in the chair before the desk. Nuri's pleasure was evident on his lips.

Nuri motioned for him to sit, then took out the ledger. He opened a side desk drawer, searching for cheque-books. 'One moment,' he said. He laid one down and brushed his hand across the cover. 'I am ready,' he said. 'Do not worry.'

'Mr Nuri,' Ben said, glancing up at him and unfastening the black briefcase. Perhaps, he thought, they know something else about the revolution. He often wondered if they would tell him when the Shah came to L.A. Maybe they were thinking of going back.

'Yes? You have something, Mr Ben?'

'I heard that you're closing the car company. Is that true?'

Nuri leaned back his head and took off his glasses. He laid them on the desk. 'The automobiles, yes. Today, I tell Julian. He must.'

'Patrick said you might close the bakeries, too.'

Nuri said nothing. He opened the cheque-book in front of him. 'If we lose money, we will have to.'

'But Mr Nuri – '

He hushed him with his hands. 'It is not for you, Mr Ben. It is for Julian. He listens to Freddy blah blah blah. Freddy! What he know? I ask you.'

'He doesn't know anything.'

'Exactly.'

'Julian shouldn't listen to him.'

'What he does? Julian, he listens to everybody. I tell him before he start he lacks the experience in these businesses. He must close them. But Mr Ben, you – you are friend to me and to Julian. We are grateful to you.'

'Well, thank you.'

'Yes, we thank you.' He rubbed the lenses of his glasses with a kleenex. 'Mr Ben, perhaps when we go back, you will go with us. You can work in the businesses there. Do not worry. Julian and I, we trust you.'

My God, Ben thought, listening. He tried to smile, but the thought of going to Iran . . .

'Or if we stay – '

'What would you do with the bakeries if you left?' Ben asked.

'We will close them. For what do we need them?' Ben could hardly believe him. Why did you start them, then, he wanted to ask. No one told us you might close so soon.

'The bakeries will make money. They're making a profit now. Maybe Valley Mall is losing, not Westwood.'

Mr Nuri put on his glasses and shook his head. 'No. I tell Julian over and over.' He opened the manila-covered notebook. 'For February, Mr Ben. You see. The income, she is so. Yes? The figures you gave me. Look for yourself.'

It was evident he would not let himself be convinced.

'All right.' Ben leaned across. The figures were all in Nuri's handwriting.

'And the expenditures. Here.' He held his fingernail just under the total.

'No.' Ben shook his head. 'What are you counting? Look – ' He turned the notebook around to face him. 'Mr Nuri, some of these entries are from months before the bakery opened. Not from now.' He began to read the entries aloud. 'What's this $3,000 for a sign? We didn't buy a sign since I've been here.'

'What does it matter – a month, two month, four month ago? Julian he pay. It is the same. He loses every month. For February, for March, for April. Eh? I subtract the income from the expenditures. Who cares, if he loses, Mr Ben? No one.'

'I care. I'm the manager.'

'Yes. You care. But who else? It is not only the bakeries.' Nuri began to count off on his fingers. 'Julian he lose five thousand a month for them, six thousand for the boutique, eight thousand for the automobile, five thousand for the suntan. He put over a million dollars into them. In Iran it is a *lot* of money. He loses one hundred fifty thousand each month.'

'How could he?'

'For the business in Teheran! She is closed, but he must pay the employees. What can they do? There is no work for them.'

'One hundred fifty thousand?' Ben shook his head, frowning. Was it possible? He wondered how much money Julian really had. 'But he can earn money on the bakeries. He can make – one hundred thousand a year at least. He has to give them a chance. They've just opened!'

'Maybe yes, Mr Ben. If he can. You tell me. It is wonderful if he can make the money.'

'I could make the bakeries profitable,' he said. 'Everything was too high to begin with. There are too many employees. Too much was paid for the equipment.' He felt his hands shaking. Go ahead, he thought. Tell him the truth. 'Why was the equipment bought in New York rather than Los Angeles?

It had to be shipped here. And it isn't even up to inspection.' He hesitated. Don't mention Abe, he thought. 'No one cared if the business would make a profit. There were too many expenses to begin with.'

'Yes?' Nuri patted his hand on the desktop. He nodded.

'People have taken advantage of Julian.'

'Yes, I agree with you.'

'But it's *business*. You must change it now or you'll lose the investment.'

'Then change them. You are manager, Mr Ben. No one, not Freddy, not Julian, not Mr Nuri.' He raised his voice. 'You are.'

'I can make them profitable,' Ben said. 'I can, if you let me.'

'It is so. I believe you. Do it. Make them regular.'

'Well, I will,' Ben said. He leaned back, forgetting why he had come in the first place. 'Don't close them,' he said.

'You are in charge,' Nuri said. 'If the bakeries lose the money, we have to close them. We have one month, two months.'

'You won't have to.'

'I am so glad for you and Julian. Do it, Mr Ben. Do not ask anyone. You are in charge. I will tell Julian today. If you want that we do not go by, we will not. You will make the business regular. You must do it if you can.'

'No, no. I want you to come.'

'It is so,' Mr Nuri said. 'Julian, he is very worried. He does not know what to do. He must not lose more money.'

Ben began to organize the moment he left Nuri. He would take an hour first and go back to Westwood before his appointment with Elaine. He would make a list of ways to save money. Then how to increase income. Downstairs, he glanced at the spread-out orange fins of the pickup, the tail lights on. Someone inside pressed his foot on the brakes.

Patrick raised his eyebrows and pointed toward the customer.

'Is he interested in buying it?' Ben asked. He noticed the Iranian adjusting the seat, then turning the steering wheel.

67

'Who knows? Did you get bad news?'

'No.'

Patrick shrugged. 'You going to Westwood?'

'Yes.'

He nodded as if it were all right.

Ben opened the glass doors, aware of how dimly lighted the showroom was. He walked to his car and got in. It started with the radio on, and he rolled down the window, sunshine in his eyes. It gleamed on the dash and against the bright white hood. OK. Write everything down. Make the choices, then see what's best. Get the point clear. He let out on the clutch and started along Westwood. He turned right, down Kelton. He liked Nuri's making him boss. Here's your chance, he thought. You don't own anything, but you can run this business as if it were yours. That's an opportunity you couldn't find anywhere else.

Didn't you think you'd do better so far? he asked himself. Honestly? Shouldn't all these problems be cleared up? Abe said there'd be nothing to do in a month. Maybe you're not as good as you thought.

He didn't accept that.

He drove to Westwood and parked in the loading zone. He walked past the front, looking in at Anya, Maurice, and Madeleine. He nodded to Maurice, then continued to the back door. When he opened it, Ramon glanced up. Don't let them know that anything has changed, he thought.

But it had.

Money had made the whole business flinch. Like profit was a whip, and the bakery had better listen. We've got a new master, Ben wanted to say. It's not rich Julian. Certainly it's not me. It's money. And it's hard. It means business. If I don't, it does. So watch out.

Ramon's face was sweaty. The work was harder than Ben could have imagined. Wasn't baking what women did in kitchens? Ramon could have been hauling furniture for all the strain. His pride made his round face more shiny. He didn't want bothered. All he needed in a kitchen were the ingredients, a few pans, and an oven. He didn't *ever* need to be told *anything*. Wasn't that a kind of responsibility? It was. And so was his own, watching each of them.

Are we all responsible for the bakery's making money? If Julian thought of closing, did it mean everyone was to blame? He thought so. Because they had all wanted as much of Julian's money as they could get.

'Ben,' Ramon said, rolling a stack of trays toward the refrigerator. 'Can I show you something?'

Ben followed him to the refrigerator and walked inside. The cool mousses already had white marshmallow circles on top, and the cheesecakes, the chocolate creams lined the metal racks. The bakers had been busy. Ramon pointed to a cake that was magic with steam, cooling. The cake was the size of a wagon wheel.

'It's a special order, he said. 'I'm not supposed to do special orders. I want overtime to finish it. And for cleaning. Jose's boy is sick, and Jose can't clean.'

'You're on salary,' Ben said. 'Just like I am.'

Ben left the refrigerator, his arms cold.

He sat at a table in the front and turned to a blank page in his notebook. There were two Westwood bakers for bread, Ramon and Jose. One for croissants, Scott, and an assistant. Plus the fancy pastry chef since Lars had quit. Ramon made six hundred a week, the pastry chef six hundred, the others three hundred fifty each. He wrote down the names, then crossed out two. Saving nine hundred fifty dollars a week. Didn't that make sense?

We don't even sell a hundred dollars' worth of bread a week, he thought. Quit baking it. Bake more light pastries, sweet rolls, brownies, large chocolate cookies. They'll sell. Ramon should go, and Scott's assistant. Ben got up, filled a cup with coke and sat down. He drank, then kept ice in his mouth. Abe wouldn't agree; he would fight it. He insisted that the bread was important. He's your friend, Ben thought. He hired you. If he cheated Julian, it's not your business.

Julian will have to decide. Tell him no bread. Two bakers at Westwood, with a bake off just before the bakers leave every day. He began to chew on the top of the plastic pen. You'll have to show Julian what the changes would mean.

'Oh Ben,' Maurice said. 'It is business you think of, no?'

He glanced up at him. Cut Maurice too, he thought.

'You imagine how much money the bakery will make, huh?'

'Do you think it makes money?' he asked. 'How much?'

'Ahh. How much? How many dollars?' Maurice's voice was exaggerated.

'They pay your salary, Maurice.'

'So they are most important, yes? As nothing else is? Not people in your novel? Or my songs? It is so important?'

'OK,' Ben said, glancing at the clock. 'What do you want to talk about? We have five minutes.'

Maurice scooted back the chair and sat down beside him. He hadn't shaved. He kept his nails long for playing the guitar. 'Ahh, there is hope,' he said. 'I have good news to tell you. I am so lucky.' He leaned closer, looking very worried. 'Last night Madeleine and I went to a cabaret here. I met this guy who asked me to sing. He listened to my songs and he will help produce them. He has experience in the business.'

Ben could see the pulse beating in Maurice's thin neck.

'I like them, too,' Ben said, waiting.

'But I need a little money – to rent a studio for one afternoon.' His voice was hardly audible. He cleared his throat. 'And for a back up on the guitar.'

'I don't have money to give you.'

'No – I will ask Freddy for it. Five hundred dollars is nothing to him. What do you think?'

'Why should he loan you money?' Ben said. 'What if he said no? You'd get angry. Wait a while, then ask.'

'He has to. It is nothing to him. I will ask him when he comes in.' Maurice couldn't sit still. He rubbed his arms, then the hair across his skinny chest. He began to rub his fingertips against his forehead.

The profit was like the thinnest glaze on a cake. It was never obvious. If it seemed to be everywhere, it never was. Certainly not in the cash register bell or in the bright pastries. The money was in some method that made the difference between what was taken in and what was spent. It was always a gamble. To make money, he thought, you can't listen to people.

There was no need for three people at the counter, Ben thought. No matter what Abe said. He wrote down the names. Cut back to one at a time. Pay a little more so that no one complained if they got too busy. He wrote down the amount for keeping one helper during the lighter time of the day, and two at breakfast, lunch, and dinner.

The ingredients were next. Don't try to make a profit by using too little or the wrong ones, but don't allow waste. He wondered how much a single croissant cost. Or a piece of cake. A mousse? Everything cost something. He did, the milk, the lights, the front door. Time did. Nothing should be wasted.

Why weren't businesses made of joy? So that if a man loved to bake, then he did it, and opened a store where he gave away his work. Think of his profit.

Maurice and Madeleine should be cut. And probably Elaine. Definitely Ramon.

It was nearly twelve o'clock by his watch. He calculated that he could save the bakery eighteen hundred dollars a week for starters. Maurice should go, Madeleine, Ramon, and Elaine. The products that were usually thrown away could be sold half price. Only a little bread should be made. All the baking should be done at Westwood. Just turn off the expensive ovens at Valley Mall. It would either work or be a disaster. And everything would be changed. These people gave it the very character that made the business lose money. He would have to get rid of them. Even the ones he hired.

He listened inside himself for a minute. Wasn't he saying to make the bakeries like all the others? To conserve first? To change everything Abe had tried to do differently? But you like him. You don't even know what is Abe's fault. You've only been working two months.

He was aware that Maurice watched him, and Madeleine looked over her shoulder as she swept. Anya sat behind the register and waited for the next customer. They thought that he was too quiet.

He glanced outside the window.

Don't you care about them? he thought. About Maurice and Madeleine? Or Ramon and his wife and babies? Or Elaine?

Of course I care.

They were hired just like you were.

He sat a moment, an intimate voice nudging him.

How would you like to be fired?

That's different. I wouldn't mind.

He looked outside at the traffic. Was that true?

Yes. I could write. I'd be relieved to get away.

But they wouldn't be. And *you'd* have to stay.

He hadn't thought of that. Would he be locking himself in? For how long?

He didn't know. A long time. Until everything ran smoothly.

He sat back, frowning. If he stayed, he could save more money from his salary. But there would be one problem after another. They wouldn't end no matter how many he solved. His job was to deal with problems.

Suddenly he couldn't hear anything inside the bakery. His world lit up, from the bright sunlight outside and his thoughts. He didn't want to face a single other problem the bakery had.

Do you have to? You have money in the bank. Just tell Julian how you think things should be changed. Leave after you promised Abe.

You can't fire them if you're not going to stay.

A car sped by. He recognized Freddy and his blonde girlfriend. Freddy waved, seeing him.

Let Freddy run the stores, he thought. They're his.

There are always other jobs.

He waited a moment. Oh there were. And the jobs lay on the other side of quitting. They were like cards, in a game. Weren't they?

He could feel chill bumps on his arms.

Was it possible?

He pushed back his chair. He hadn't thought about it before. But he could leave. Couldn't everyone? Wasn't that kind of freedom always there? People just got covered up by work, like bugs under logs.

He liked himself for the first time since he had talked to Nuri. Everything could be put into Julian's hands. He didn't know how much money Julian had. Or how he wanted to spend it. If Julian cared most about money, he should make the decisions. Julian could start by saving the largest salary.

He looked at Maurice and Madeleine. He loved them because he was not going to fire them. He loved how they felt so strongly about things. Isn't that why they caused problems in the first place? Because they weren't all business, as he had tried to be?

Neither am I, he thought.

He breathed in, excited.

Well, can you quit? Is it all right?

He looked around the bakery, the glass just cleaned.

If you want to.

He could have sung, standing up. 'Oh Maurice,' he said. 'Are you determined to ask Freddy for the money?' He had been afraid that Maurice would ask him for it.

'When he comes in.' Maurice stiffened, his face stubborn.

'Listen,' Ben said. 'Maybe he will give it to you. I'll ask him myself if you want.'

'Would you ask him first?'

'He might listen,' Ben said. He had to smile at Madeleine who put her arms around him. Her lips were coloured like flowers, and smelled of roses.

'I am so sorry, Ben,' she said, 'for everything I said about you. Will you ask? Please?'

'Of course I will.' The front door opened. The sunshine beamed on to the red tile. What can you give away? he thought. And he went into the back. Ramon was gone. He hadn't washed the pans, and the floor was sticky with flour. It didn't matter. If he ever wanted to, it would be something he could talk about.

Ben went back to the front. He would take Elaine a present. He would tell everyone to work extra hard. When he thought of what he almost had done!

He saw Nuri, just outside the bakery. Go on, he thought. Tell him you want to meet. Ben hurried out to see him. Nuri stood close to the curb. He would meet with them and give his suggestions.

'Mr Nuri,' he said. 'Come in. It is too windy.'

'I am awaiting Julian, Mr Ben. How are you?'

'Can we meet tomorrow? With Julian?'

'Of course. I will tell him.'

'At ten?'

'When Julian is agreeable,' he said. 'Do not worry.'

The limousine pulled up and Ben opened the door for Mr Nuri. Nuri got in, then Ben closed it. Their lives were safe inside the soft upholstered car. Julian waved. He was watching television. I love you too, Ben thought. But you shouldn't be so showy. Not with all the feeling against Iran. He watched the car pull out; he turned around and went back into Le Champs. For a moment, he again saw Julian's face in front of the television.

Ben hesitated, then took a card from his wallet and looked at it.

Union Gold Corporation. He would call Mr Freeman about working for him. Maybe he already had another job. But was that fair? he asked. If you have another job and the others don't?

It was hard, but wasn't it fair? He thought so, and he looked at the cakes, the delicate mousses, the fine breads . . . it was a parade, wasn't it? He let himself be happy.

Julian held the typed pages rather as he would a receiver if the telephone call was for someone else. His eyes looked at them from top to bottom, then back to Ben.

'I'll go over the points.' Ben started to read. 'The first page lists different ways that we can conserve expenses, including cutting out several full-time workers.' Neither Nuri nor Julian looked at the paper or at him. Julian picked at the lint on the knee of his trousers, then shuffled the pages.

Ben read on. He could see that Nuri was smiling. The more he read, the bigger the smile. Yes, we are agreed, Ben thought. You and I see alike. We know how to run a business.

'The kitchen has never been organized, and we should stop now, use our inventory and start over. By the end of this month we should have an estimate not only of supply costs but how much each product costs us. We will be better able to know how much to charge.'

Nuri took off his glasses, and his eyes were shining. Thank you, thank you, he said without speaking.

'We need to change to registers that are more accurate and simple to use.'

Julian turned to the last page when Ben still discussed the first.

'Are there questions so far? I know it's a radical change.'

Julian seemed to move his fingertips quickly, nothing else. 'You are sure of these figures?' he asked.

'I'm sure of the ones on the paper. We need better organization if the bakeries are going to make money. If we don't care about profit, I don't suggest anything. But if we change, there's still a risk.'

'No, no. It is important, you see. A business should make the profit.' Julian's voice became shrill. 'Otherwise, how are we to run?'

'Well, you can make money from them. I'll read on.'

Julian laid down the paper and looked out the window behind the building. Mr Nuri nodded, his hand against his forehead.

When Ben stopped, Mr Nuri looked up. 'It is very good,' Nuri said.

Julian only looked tired.

'What do you think of it?' Ben asked him.

'I think yes,' Julian said, rubbing his finger against his nose.

'Another way to save money is to eliminate my job,' Ben said. 'You know my salary.'

Julian looked at Nuri as if he didn't.

'I'll stay the period I promised Abe, then I have to leave. That's one more month.'

'But Ben – ' Julian began.

Mr Nuri spoke up quickly. 'Ahh,' he said. 'I understand. For the money, yes? You will want more salary when you change. Julian and I we will talk about it later.'

'No. It isn't money.' He could see the tip of Nuri's tongue. It knows how to click, he thought. But no, could he change his mind?

'Come to dinner tonight,' Julian said. 'At my house. At eight o'clock? Is that convenient for you?'

'I'll be glad to,' Ben said.

'It is so kind of you,' Nuri said. And he nodded, barely, then glanced toward Julian. 'Do not worry,' he said. He began to talk Persian, his voice strong. Then he stopped.

'He will tell you tonight,' Nuri said.

7

Ben sat on the sofa in Julian's living room. The arms reflected bulbs of overhead light, yet a faded needlepoint depicted scenes of a ballroom. The French inhabitants of the upholstery wore white wigs and silk costumes. The gilt sofa and chairs were like furniture in an Iranian museum.

Mr Nuri waited across from him and didn't speak. He bent over in the small chair and eyed the carpet. He was listening to every word that Julian said on the telephone.

Rose carried a silver tray of sandwiches made of white bread. She set folded napkins and wine glasses on the carved table in front of him.

'Julian doesn't like sandwiches,' she whispered, 'but I got back fifteen minutes ago from San Diego. He didn't say you were coming.'

'What did you do?' Ben asked.

'I got away,' she said. 'I can't stay here very long at a time.' When she set down the tray, the dark emerald around her neck swung out. It was the size of her eyes. 'San Diego has the only beaches where I can relax. Of course it's too cold now. But it is beautiful.'

Julian's voice rose, then waited for a reply. Mr Nuri began to massage his forehead. Rose looked across the room at Julian talking.

He shouted something in Persian that caused both Rose and Nuri to glance up, at each other. Julian shouted louder. Nuri began to shake his head.

Because I am in the room, am I a part of this conversation?

Ben wondered. Don't act uncomfortable. He tried to look as if he, too, knew Persian. For himself.

Suddenly Julian cursed and hung up. Mr Nuri sat erect in his chair, his lips smiling. Rose had left the room.

Julian sat in a chair beside the sofa. He flattened the silver ascot he wore. Up close, he hadn't shaved. Under the lights, his face appeared a little fat. 'Excuse me,' he said. 'I was talking to Freddy. Would you have wine, Ben?' He poured for himself, then began to fill another glass.

Ben glanced at Nuri then away. 'I like the furniture,' he said. 'Is it Louis XIV?'

'Louis XV.' Julian poured another glass of the wine. He took a moment longer. 'Rose and I bought them in Paris over twenty years ago. They are very expensive.'

'Yes, I can see that.'

'I pay over one hundred and fifty thousand dollars for the three pieces, then.'

'Yes.' Ben raised his back slightly. 'Who did the tapestry?' he asked.

'Gobelin. Yes. They are *all* real.'

'And you got them out of Iran?'

Julian looked like a cat, pleased, then breathed in deeply.

'Here,' Ben said, pointing to the sandwiches. 'Will you have one?' He held the tray, then carried it to Nuri. Nuri took half a sandwich and laid it on his napkin. Ben sat back down, in the centre of the sofa. He took a sandwich himself.

'Ben,' Julian said, his voice high. 'Mr Nuri and I have talked of you. You know how highly he thinks of you. And I, too. I speak for both of us. For the family. Rose and Freddy.'

'I think highly of you, too,' Ben said.

'I have spent a lot of money on the businesses. It is over two million dollars already.' His voice was shrill.

Ben waited. He would say no to this offer. 'You could have made a lot just investing it,' he said.

'Yes. I lose it already.' Julian tasted the wine, then sat back.

'You haven't lost it,' Ben said.

Julian looked as if he thought he had.

Maybe so, Ben thought. He felt an uneasiness with Julian that he didn't have with Nuri.

Julian picked up another sandwich and began to eat. His large gold front tooth shone wet. He chewed, not talking, then put another sandwich on his plate. The plate had a floral design in various shades of gold.

'Mr Ben,' Nuri said. 'As Julian say to you, we are grateful for the work. I go in the morning and you are there. At lunch you are at Valley Mall. At night, Westwood. We need you. You are for the business important. We will do what you say for the bakeries. And Julian and I – ' he hesitated, 'we will ask something of you.'

Ben listened, wondering what was the most they would offer.

'All the businesses they are bad. The automobile, the boutique, the suntan, the apartments. Julian I tell you close them. It is not the business of our experience. Julian has a lot of money in them as he say.' Nuri's thin face grew tight. He licked his lips quickly. 'Julian, he asks you to take more of the business. Not at once. The boutique. Maybe the suntan, the automobile. It will be as you can do it.'

'I – '

'Wait a minute. Julian, he must close these businesses if he loses more money. His friends have trouble and look up to him. Julian he is generous to them. It is important: Julian does not want to close them. I say close them now.'

'Mr Nur – '

He shook his fingers, continuing. 'For your money,' he said. 'I talk to Julian. *No one in the family will know your salary*. It will be from an account in . . .'

Suddenly Persian started from Julian. He gestured as he spoke, then leaned back.

Nuri turned to face him. He spoke more loudly, the Persian exploding. He enunciated, in high tones, his voice determined.

Julian cut in. Ben understood *no*, then watched Julian's nervous fingers. Julian's face began to redden.

Don't argue about me, he wanted to say.

Nuri shook his head angrily. He raised his voice, and spun around. He glanced at Ben.

Julian slapped the table before him and began to shout.

Suddenly Nuri took off his glasses. The skin around his eyes was the palest white. His finger pointed and accused Julian. He shouted, louder than seemed possible. The whole room echoed. Then both were shouting.

Ben started to speak, but neither listened.

Nuri finally shook his fist, then, as he was stopping, puffed up his face. He looked at Ben to show what he thought. He looked as if he might spit. '*That dum-my*,' he said.

Ben glanced uneasily at Julian.

Julian crossed his legs at his knees. His ascot had come out of his velvet coat, and he didn't wear a shirt. He poured another glass of wine.

'I did mean what I said this morning,' Ben said. 'I've decided not to stay in business.'

'No. No.' Julian leaned back and tried to compose himself. 'You are welcome here,' he said. 'But if you wish to quit the job, I believe you.' He tasted the wine. 'There is always work here for you. We trust you.'

Julian wiped his forehead again with the napkin. 'I do not,' he said, 'know the business. I would pay you after the stores they are a success. Not now.' He nodded. 'Yes? It is OK?'

'But I can't.'

'I understand, but I am for you, Ben. You see? I do not throw good money after bad. It is not so?'

'But you have a good investment.'

'Oh it makes me tired,' Julian said. 'I hear it over and over from Abe, I lose more money when I hear it.' He finished the glass. 'I am in business over thirty years in Iran. You know thirty years? I never lose money. You do not understand. I do the business for Freddy, not for me. I am fifty-nine years old.'

'I can imagine how hard it is to leave Iran and start over.'

'It is! But I do not do it. Not for me. For Freddy. At my age I do not want to see the business every day. In Iran, I have a very big business, you see. We make millions every year.'

Ben glanced at Nuri who shook his head slowly. It was so.

'If the Minister from France comes to Teheran, he stay in my house. It is my responsibility, you see. I go everywhere in the world and my business is known. You see me, but you do not know how I feel. Here I am a stranger to everyone.'

'You can rebuild it when you go back.'

'No, it is over. I am too old now. And it is finished. I was for the American always. It is very bad in Iran.'

Ben saw Rose standing in the doorway. She looked as if she apologized for Julian.

Julian hesitated, then stopped. His breathing was audible.

Ben saw that Nuri looked sad, too. As if there was nothing else for them to do.

'It only gives both of you the opportunity to do more,' Ben said. 'To know just what you want in life.'

'I had what I want,' Julian said. 'I know. I would not take ten million dollars for what I learn. Not ten million, Ben. And I would not take one hundred million to learn it again. You understand? It is very hard.' He leaned back, against the highback chair, and seemed to sink beneath the gilt arms.

'It is yours,' Mr Nuri said. 'If you say no, then OK. You can come back if you need us.'

Ben drove home alone. The winding, tree-lined streets of Beverly Hills were black, the fenced estates lighted deep within. He could feel the wine that he had drunk. He drove fast, past Beverly Hills and into Westwood. The highrises emitted dazzling light. Down the street, he turned on Bexley and drove past the glass bakery. Maurice was just closing. Noel swept the front sidewalk, and inside, the counters were shiny. The product was put away. The red floor was mopped. The register drawer was open. Ben knew that. Oh, he thought, and for a moment he saw the *life* of Le Champs.

It is as life everywhere, he thought. It is Julian's and Nuri's and Maurice's and Ramon's and it is mine. We are all involved in it. And it is wonderful.

He pressed on the gas, passing the store. He was relieved that it was over for him. He would call Mr Freeman again, and he would begin to think the next day about what else he would do.

California Exit

I

At a Banquet

From his chair at a side table, Ben could watch Lombardi at
the dais. The dozen round tables were covered with white
banquet cloths and each had a flower centrepiece. Lombardi
had finished eating. He spread his brown fingers through his
hair, his face tanned like a sun lover. His forehead was
sweating. It was an ordeal to answer the questions that the
people nearby were asking.

Ben cut a bite from the fried chicken breast on his plate and
saw there was another dinner roll in the basket. He could tell
that Lombardi was exhausted. Who wouldn't be? You probably deserve your Nobel, he thought, looking at something
recognizably sensitive in the Italian face.

That morning Ben had shut his office door, leaned back in
his chair, put his feet on his desk, and made himself begin one
of Lombardi's novels. If he was going to meet him, he had
better read something. He had checked it as if he were a doctor
giving a private, quick examination. The prose, even trans-
lated, was hardy. The characters had interested him at once.
He had wanted to read on. He had glanced up from the page,
delighted and surprised. Then he had noticed the flickering
light on his telephone. Ben had laid down the novel and looked
outside the window at the blue city bus stopped in front of the
bank across the street. Keep the door shut, he had told
himself. Leave the phone alone. Don't bother anyone. Read all
day. He had looked down, turned another page. He remembered reading really good books. This one might well
become a classic.

Suddenly, another button had lighted on his phone. Both flickered, on hold. Don't read something good in here, he had thought. Read memos. Talk on the phone. Hold meetings. Save this for when you care about something. The intercom had buzzed, meaning that someone was waiting on the line.

He wished he hadn't come to the banquet. He glanced about the table, then took the roll. The small chandeliers made the room elegant, like Ben's suit. His tie was pulled close to his neck, and even his fingers were relaxed. He spread white butter on the roll that unfortunately was identical to those served at the faculty club.

The heavy women across the table had travelled from Turin with Lombardi and didn't know English. He gathered that they had been to a shopping mall, and he wondered which one. The dark-haired woman, Anna, was Lombardi's younger sister. He didn't remember the tall one's name. The man beside him, whose wrist showed out of the sleeves of his jacket, was Lombardi's personal secretary. He had introduced the women, with difficulty. The only person at the table who spoke English besides Ben was a member of the Italian faculty, and he would have been the last to utter a word of it. He sat like a duck in water, dousing his Italian with the cheap wine the waiters poured into their glasses.

He saw Daryl two tables over and quickly looked away. He had enough of him at work. Daryl was one administrator that Ben was certain he could not trust. Just before the banquet Daryl had called, insistent on meeting about the margins of the new course proposal form.

Ben had been silly to come. He felt his soft cotton shirt with his fingers and glanced at his watch. Nine thirty. The dinner had started nearly forty minutes late. The wine was beginning to have an effect.

Right now, he thought, you could be home, finished with dinner. You could understand what people are saying. But you're here. Lombardi might as well be on the moon. Well, what did you expect?

He cut another piece of the chicken with the edge of his knife.

The water glass left a damp circle around the bottom, on the tablecloth. A swallow of wine was left in the clear glass, and his plate, the university monogrammed silverware on it, was empty.

He began to talk to himself, like someone had let a cat out of a bag. Near his table, a red cord closed off the adjoining room. It contained sofas and tapestries from Marie Antoinette's antechamber at Versailles. Dean Williams had told him that the walls and green marble stairs were authentic replicas. The Simpsons had bought the room and furniture for themselves, then donated them to the University. Imagine, he thought. Marie Antoinette had waited to be arrested in that room and she must have been frightened that she would die. He thought of her doing needlepoint as she sat on the gilded sofa.

Often, riding home from work, he would think about the violent stories on the news in Los Angeles. That morning one reporter told about a street shooting of the niece of an eastern senator. She and her boyfriend had been leaving an excellent restaurant in Venice. He had eaten there himself. And not three blocks from where he lived, after midnight a week before, three masked gunmen held up every customer at a fast food place. They herded them into a room-sized refrigerator, then executed them one by one. The news had omitted how. He passed the restaurant on his way to school and the place still had business. Probably because of its specials on eggs. But think of being there at the moment. Which is what he did. He was tied on the floor of a van in one story, an ice pick being drilled into his head, and on his knees in a refrigerator in this one, a gun barrel against the pulse in his neck. Or he worried about Alice and Jules at home alone. A teacher in Jules's pre-school class had gone into her apartment one Wednesday after buying groceries and had found a burglar in the kitchen. The man had raped her with her three-year-old, Carey, crying. Oh he would move if anything like that happened. But it would be too late. Why take a chance? What was worth it?

Nothing, he thought. The violence was not real; it was stories on the news. They kept him a little afraid.

Across the room sat the powerful new President of the University. He looked the part, distinguished, his gaze direct. Peel had come to State with the highest recommendations.

'You are with the University?' Mr Bentilli's uneasy pronunciation hid his English. Now what about him was so Italian? In a white robe he would have looked Arabic. It would take a large effort to communicate anything.

'I head the writing programme,' Ben said. 'We're a part of the school of Lifelong Learning. We have playwrights, novelists, film writers.'

'Oh. And you write, too. Yourself?'

'Yes.' Well, he did.

'And you are part of this? Who – ' he hesitated. 'Who spon-sor it?' He leaned over, then stuck his hand in his back pocket. The wallet he took out had lira. He handed Ben a white card.

'Thank you. I – '

'To write, then. In case there is something, yes? These meetings are important, no? If you have use of me for some reason?'

'Thank you,' Ben said. He put the card in his coat pocket.

That composed his entire conversation during the meal.

Daryl caught up with him as he was walking out the high, black-painted doorway.

'Our meeting with Nona in the morning might surprise you,' Daryl said.

'Oh?' Ben tried not to show his interest.

'I shouldn't say anything.' Daryl's lips were as glossy as his forehead, perspiration in beads across it.

Ben hurried on, along the shrubbery that was being watered by the automatic sprinkler.

At Wilshire, on 26th he waited for the signal to change, the marquee bright. On the opposite corner starving mannequins in the windows of a women's boutique wore red and black peek-a-boo underwear. The signal blinked; he started, uneasy about the cars behind. He signalled left when he pressed on the gas, indicating that he was turning immediately into one of the narrow drives just off the intersection. The Mercedes behind sped around in the right lane. Ben pulled in on top of the concrete riders, and stopped at the gate.

He went up the walk to the front door. He could see through the small glass window. Alice had left on the kitchen light. He unlocked the door 'and stepped into the entry. Two white porcelain figurines were on the desk. The rented house had yellow flowered curtains that bunched. Everything was clean, the dining area too. He crossed the room and hurried through the swinging door into the kitchen. The light above the sink was on and a dishrag was left to dry over the faucet.

Ben got a glass from the cabinet and opened the refrigerator. The heavy green wine bottle felt wet around the neck. He filled the glass, then put the bottle back on the top shelf. The wine tasted cold, like water, but juicy in his mouth. He swallowed. He turned around.

Jules, in red flannel pyjamas, held up his arms. 'My legs hurt, Daddy.'

'All right, I'll rub them.' Ben picked him up in the doorway and carried him to his bed in the next room. He laid Jules on top of the blue comfort then went back into the kitchen, switched off the light, and got his glass.

Ben sat on Jules's bed, his hand on the little calves. He began to think of Daryl and Nona. She was Dean and controlled his programme. Daryl's grin meant that something unpleasant was coming. 'It's better already,' Ben said after a moment. 'Your legs hurt because you're growing.'

'They hurt a lot, Daddy.'

Alice is asleep, Ben thought. He leaned back against the pillow, then reached for the glass. Even cold, the wine was green on his tongue. Go to sleep, he told himself. The banquet had made him late and tired. Now he was worried. He had to get up at five and work on his novel before he left for work. He sipped like he was drinking from a creek, then laid back his head. He yawned, his eyelids floating over the wine.

A Meeting with Nona

State's generous public budget gave it the grandiose look of someone's well-kept mansion. Palm trees lined the sunlit walks, and the brick buildings, a mixture of old and new, identified California's past. The degrees that State had granted, the thousands of BAs and MAs and hundreds of Ph.Ds, gave it deep roots into California life. State was praised for its excellence in Engineering, Law, and Medicine as well as for its departments of Philosophy, Sociology, and English. The University was known too, for its special offerings designed for individuals who wanted to study, but had no plans to earn a degree. These non-credit courses flowered into cooking, culture, and aerobics classes. The non-credit offerings made it possible for anyone, at little cost, to attend a class at State.

Writers who came to Ben by way of the programme were testimony to the vagaries of a writing career: novelists, playwrights, screenwriters, article writers, reviewers, gift card writers, writers for animation, research writers, technical business writers, diarists, newspaper writers, song writers, librettists.

He was in charge of the large department. He was responsible for making sure that none of the courses in his division – credit or non-credit – lost money. The programme drew students nationwide and hired two dozen writers to teach them in seminars. It had an excellent reputation.

He parked, and watching the clock tower which could be seen from all parts of campus, walked to the Dean of Lifelong Learning's office. Nona Weygand was the most powerful woman in the university and had her hands on the controls of chairing search committees for vice presidents, the deans and chairmen. No one had given her power; she had taken it. In five years she had tripled the college expenditures, usually at the expense of others, expanded hiring, facilities, enrolment and course offerings. She had supervised the development of several new degrees and had vastly expanded credit offerings. The college was not just cooking and craft courses. It offered two Master's, several B.A.'s, and affected the entire university.

She said what she meant with the directness of a pointed finger. There was no question of her authority – she kept it sharpened like a tongue. When she spoke, the warning in her voice was that of an experienced teacher known for being hard. Nona was a leader.

She put on lipstick at her desk. She gave Ben the impression that she was tugging at her girdle, her clover green dress an expensive old one. She must have worn it many times. She cleared her throat, a kleenex in her knuckles. 'Take a seat, Ben. I'm coming.'

He placed the manila folders on the table then saw her pull at a desk drawer, take out something and push the drawer closed. She put a cough drop in her mouth.

'Daryl's coming from Milt's office.' She walked from the desk to the open door and motioned to Fay. 'Would you like coffee, Ben? Make it one, Fay. And one hot tea.' Her cough sounded bad. She dabbed her nose, then pulled out the armchair at the oak table. She sipped from the water glass in front of her.

Fay was sorry, but Dean Arnold was on the line.

'You told him I was in conference?' Nona was surprised. 'One minute, Ben.' She crossed the room to her desk, took off her silver earring and picked up the receiver. 'Bill, I'm about to start a meeting,' she said. She listened. 'I understood that Guy had signed off already.' She was not used to being interrupted. 'Well.' Her brows raised, she brought the kleenex to her nose. 'Could I call you on this – I'm sure that's the case. No, I'll call you.'

When she had hung up, she crossed the room and sat down. She looked at Ben, her cheeks red. 'He called me "my dear," ' she said. 'My dear, I heard that you've proposed a course in translation.' She slid the cough drop under her tongue, then against her cheek. 'What was I supposed to say to that?'

'He didn't mean anything,' Ben said, surprised she'd tell him.

'Of course he did.' She let out a long breath, and cleared her throat. She looked up just as Ben did.

Ben evened the edges of the papers in the folder in front of him.

Daryl brought his own mug full of coffee. He set it on the table, then opened his briefcase. The files inside were colour coded. His striped red and white tie looked as wide as it was long. He sat down and began to blow on the coffee.

Nona looked at the thin watch on her wrist. 'Start off with your report,' she said. 'In my eyes, these are a manager's production report.'

Oh? Her attitude toward certain academic things affected Ben like a bad odour. He refused to think of a college like a factory, even for management. 'Do you want to talk about the translation course first?' he asked.

Nona glanced up at him. 'Go ahead with your report.'

Ben looked at both of them nervously. Their fingers were already on the shiny penny he'd brought them.

He opened the folder and quite unexpectedly had all the pots and pans out of his head. He hadn't meant to. 'You know that I've hired three Academy Award winners to teach.' He listed them although they knew. 'It's brought publicity, but better, it's been most popular with students.' He passed over giving an example.

Nona looked directly at him while she squeezed her nose with the kleenex.

'To make money in education,' he said, 'you find valuable minds. To make a million dollars you find a million-dollar mind. I think that's what we're doing.' Ben thought that he was good at being vulgar and that they loved it. It came naturally to him. But it was not his best quality.

Daryl's forehead shone as he leaned, grinning, under the overhead light.

'I'd like to develop a series of writing classes *all* taught by Academy Award winners.' He could see at once that Nona liked it. 'We couldn't miss. We'd call it the Academy Award Series and run a full page ad in the *Times* with half a page one word: Quality.' He hesitated for emphasis.

'The publicity would be prestigious for us and the faculty. We could be selective in whom we admit. The courses could have credit and non-credit tracks. This series could attract everyone,' he said. 'It would make money.'

'And could you recruit faculty from your contacts already?' Daryl asked.

Ben nodded. 'It wouldn't cost much,' he added. 'We've already hired the best.'

'I don't see why not then,' Nona said. She laid down her yellow pencil. 'What do you think, Daryl?'

'I think so.' He chuckled, his stomach straining his shirt.

'Let's continue,' Nona said.

Ben leaned back, his chair squeaking. 'Twenty-one of our ninety applicants for next year are Phi Beta Kappa. And they are from good schools – Wellesley, Texas, Virginia, Stanford . . .' He had several others if he needed them. 'Wisconsin, Michigan. The student academic profile is vastly improved.'

Nona looked like she wasn't sure if she'd take a bite. He gave her a moment longer. It's true, try me, he thought. You don't believe it? And I'm responsible for the improvement.

She cleared her throat. 'I'm glad this meeting was already scheduled because I wanted to meet with you anyway.' Her tone of voice changed.

He glanced up, surprised. She was unhappy about something. Daryl was right.

'You know we have a Lifelong College deficit – but you don't know the size. It's over three million dollars this year. That's twice as high as it has ever been. We are being forced to deal with that ourselves by President Peel.' She sipped the hot tea. 'He insists on changes to prevent it in the future.'

'Oh,' Ben said. He had heard that Nona had problems with Peel.

'Our new President is concerned with the extent of our credit courses, and about our sponsoring degrees.' She cleared her throat, her eyes just showing emotion.

'But continuing education here always has been unusual,' Ben said.

'He has strong preferences regarding us. I don't know to what extent he can put his ideas into effect. But he insists that all our programmes must become more traditional continuing education.'

'You mean part-time students and non-credit classes?'

Nona hesitated. 'Right now I don't know if we even want Phi Beta Kappas. We want older writers coming back to school part time.'

'The Dean doesn't mean that we don't want Phi Beta Kappas.' Daryl said. 'She means that a Phi Beta Kappa coming back to take a class or two is fine. We don't want new students who just graduated and are going directly to graduate school full time.'

'But that's ninety-nine per cent of the programme.'

'Until you've gotten the facts, you don't know what per cent it is,' Nona said.

'But non-credit has never been the emphasis. It is on quality credit graduate education.' That was why he took the job in the first place. It had always been unusual to have a graduate programme in a School of Lifelong Learning.

Nona cleared her throat, her voice weakening. 'There's a

possibility President Peel will try to move several programmes, including yours, if we don't alter them slightly and justify their being in continuing education. The new emphasis should be on non-credit.'

'But we're successful as we are – and very profitable.'

'Go ahead with your report,' Nona said. 'I probably shouldn't have said anything. Not now.'

Daryl tried to encourage him by moving his eyebrows.

'The programme can't support itself on non-credit and part-time,' he said. Neither Nona nor Daryl spoke.

Shut up, Ben thought. You won't prove anything by an out and out argument. You don't know what she is up to.

Nona took another cough drop. She motioned toward the papers in front of them.

'The proposed budget was $425,000,' he said. 'See page three. We enrolled 170 students each term and our income was $545,000.' He waited for them to turn to the chart. 'I cut expenses as detailed on page four. Our profit was $110,000. Three years ago when I came here, the programme lost $68,000. That's a $178,000 improvement. So far, none of the profit has been fed into the programme – not one dollar.'

Nona sighed then turned to the next page. She nodded, her mouth pursed. 'I don't have any difficulties with your income, Ben. I just wish I could say the same for some others.'

Daryl spoke up quickly. 'I've heard the Dean compliment it several times before her advisory board.'

'We'll all have to cut back and help the deficit more,' Nona said.

'Is the President thinking of pulling all credit courses from the college?' Ben asked.

Nona nodded slowly, then changed her mind.

Again, neither she nor Daryl spoke. There were nearly 1,500 credit courses in the college. Almost every course in his programme was a credit one. All the profitable ones were. The problem was serious for all of them.

If another college took the credit courses, his programme could not exist. One per cent of the income would be left. When the university offered a credit class, tuition was $1,500. Each non-credit class was only $200 to $250. There was money in credit education, none in non-credit. If there had been a burglar alarm in the College of Lifelong Learning, it would have been ringing loudly.

His programme would have to move to another part of the university. So would he.

And Nona wouldn't allow it.

'Several other parts of the university want the programme,' he said. 'They've hinted – '

Nona's eyes flashed. She tightened her lips, angrily. 'You work for *me*,' she said. 'I hired you.'

His leash was just as long as the amount of profit his programme made for them. Given the emergency, his programme meant nothing to her. She would ruin it rather than give it up. Change the whole thing. Advertise it with cooking courses. She would never let it go if she could help it. And why should she? She had built an academic empire and it was partly hers.

'I've asked Daryl to meet with you,' she said.

Daryl nodded slowly.

'Daryl has experience with programmes where cutting is essential. He will report to me. I think that's all I have time for this morning. We'll meet regularly.'

Ben pushed back his chair from the conference table, took a deep breath and started out. Nona followed, speaking in a low voice to Fay at the doorway.

'Wait up,' Daryl said.

Ben looked at his watch quickly.

'I have a couple of things for you,' Daryl said.

He didn't want Daryl telling him what to do. If he had an open shot at Nona, he could persuade her about policy, until her lips softened and she gave in. Like a punctured tyre letting out hot air.

He looked at Daryl's silver knit shirt that was soft enough to pop, too, the material tight at the white buttons. Nona blew her nose softly. She glanced at Ben and smiled.

Daryl stepped down into the convention entrance of the building. Ben opened one of the wide glass doors.

Daryl took his arms out of the plaid jacket and folded it. 'Don't listen to everything Nona says. Some of her comments aren't what she means.' He winked, like it wasn't important. 'When she's worried – '

'She shouldn't say she doesn't want Phi Beta Kappas,' Ben said. He started down the sidewalk that passed the tennis courts.

'I agree with you.'

'And she may as well know she can't change this into a non-credit programme.' He glanced at Daryl. It's ridiculous, he thought. Tell her. I want her to know. 'Non-credit and part-time account for one per cent of the budget. Do you agree with her?'

Daryl unbuttoned the tight collar under his tie. 'Sometimes my role is to talk things over with people.' He set down his briefcase and wiped his face with a kleenex he took from his pocket. 'Can you have lunch now?'

'No. And I want you and Nona both to know that you've taken all the money out of it that you can.'

Daryl's face showed his effort to control himself.

'If you think for a minute that other colleges in the university won't jump at the chance to have it, you're wrong. I can take it to another college.'

'No, you can't. Nona would fire you the minute you tried. I'm talking about small changes at first, Ben. Sometimes I've noticed that your office isn't open at eight.'

'I won't hear it.'

'And we should meet soon about how much you pay faculty.'

'They're prominent writers,' Ben said, 'and they make nothing.' He heard his voice begin to shake.

'Calm down. I mean small cuts that you and I can discuss. Yours isn't the only budget that's getting reduced. Frankly, you're lucky we're not thinking of more now. No one has suggested your job.'

'Mine makes money.'

'Others that we're cutting do, too.'

Ben nodded. He began to walk faster. 'Try cutting the ones that lose,' he said.

'Take your xerox bill,' Daryl said.

'You'll lose the hundred thousand profit if you start that,' Ben said. 'I have to go, Daryl.' He turned toward Journalism, away from the six-storey building. The sidewalk was cracked and the grass a bright, deep green. Ben stared up at the windows of the Dean's office.

He hurried in the opposite direction, passing students going to class. The bell in the library clock tower began to ring noon. He continued past the student centre.

Of course she could fire him.

He walked under the even row of palms, toward the student centre. At the red brick building, he went in and climbed the one flight of stairs. He was out of breath at the top.

He would care very much if she did.

Ben stepped into the narrow telephone booth and put in a quarter and dialled. He waited for Alice to answer. On the fifth ring, he hung up.

In one area his authority matched Nona's. He knew the programme itself, the students, courses, the politics and finances. She could ask him questions, but the answers were in his experience. She couldn't remove what he knew about how things were run. Or whom he was friends with in the administration. He had written the curriculum, hired the faculty, admitted the students, brought in and spent the money. Her power was to oversee. Each of them had an independence.

But if you try to move the programme on your own, he thought, if another department wants you and meanwhile Nona fires you?

Who is going to jump in after you?

3

At the Office

Ben picked out the key as he hurried up the stairs to his office. In the hallway, he fitted it into the lock then quietly shut the door. He sat in the chair and leaned back. The glow coming between the venetian blinds would disappear when he turned on the overhead light. He rubbed his eyelids and yawned. Take a minute if you want, he thought. He looked down at his desk. He tried to make everything obvious. He put memos he needed on top as well as books he should be reading, manuscripts, phone messages, schedules.

He tried to decide whether or not to make an appointment with Vice President Pilkington. He could tell him confidentially what Nona was trying to do to his programme. He could suggest its being moved.

He picked up the phone and tried Alice again. No answer.

He was startled as Chuck knocked loudly and opened the door.

Chuck flicked on the switch, flooding the room. 'I didn't know you were here,' he said. 'I'm sorry. Do you want the light off?'

'No, that's fine. Could you – '

'Howard Israel just called from Dallas and a student's been waiting since noon,' Chuck said. 'Sylvia didn't tell me she made an appointment. She forgot she wasn't supposed to.' Chuck leaned down, his brows raised. 'I've told him you were busy. Do you want me to make it for another time?'

'No. Bring his file first. Then send him in.' Ben hesitated. 'And would you get Vice President Pilkington's secretary on the phone afterwards?'

'Sure. I told Mr Israel you'd call him back.'

He wished he hadn't said he'd see him when he saw the student's name. If he had known it was Lester, he would have rescheduled rather than met with him.

Lester sat down in the yellow upholstered chair. He began to talk at once. 'I ca-came by twice yesterday, but of course you weren't in. I wanted to talk with you.'

Ben opened the file, nodding. He certainly had been in.

He remembered a particular recommendation in Lester's file. 'Under no circumstances should Tim Lester teach. And I have serious doubts about *any* writing programme admitting him.' The words surprised him every time. Wouldn't he have told someone no when they asked for a recommendation?

He turned pages, but couldn't find it.

Lester cleared his throat. 'Anyway, I don't have time to talk now.' He glanced at his watch. 'My appointment was for noon.'

He's forty-one, Ben saw, two years older than I am.

'I think we need a major in writing daytime television melodrama.'

Anyone who knew Ben would have noticed his nose. He felt it stiffen a little. 'Soap operas?'

'You should let the students vote on courses,' Lester said. 'You see, I want to make *money* writing. I'm not paying $6,000 tuition to write like Shakespeare.'

'I don't think you do,' Ben said. 'No one does, do they?' He wondered if Sylvia had made the appointment on purpose. He thought of her purple velvet slacks, a brass bull's head fastening her belt, the hips squooched up. The velvet slacks tucked in her yellow leather boots. 'It's difficult,' Ben said. 'I know a lot of fine writers who don't make money. Maybe it would have been different twenty years ago.' He wondered. 'Magazines used to pay thousands for a story.'

'I don't want to be Shakespeare,' Lester said firmly.

'And you aren't,' Ben said again. 'He's dead.' He sat back,

popping his knuckles. 'What we all have to care about is writing clearly, about language. The time to worry about money is if something's good.' Were they just words, he wondered? 'Our emphasis is on quality.'

'I don't know what you mean by quality,' Lester said.

He picked up the file. He wished Lester didn't smoke a pipe. It stuck out of his mouth like a tail. He tried to look at his nose rather than the goatee under it. The small nostril hairs were dark and curly. 'You remember last semester when you got here, I said that you were not actually accepted into the programme? The notice of acceptance was sent out by error?' He saw that Lester's lips just parted.

'The computer in admissions accepted people at random who were rejected and rejected people who were accepted. Your GRE scores – ' he pulled out the thin green sheet. He waited a moment. 'They're under 300 combined. Over half the students we admitted made 1,400 or higher.' It was fact talking. 'I let you in because you had already moved your things here from New York.'

'I thought you'd bring that up. One reason I came was to tell you I made As in both classes,' Lester said.

'Good,' Ben said quickly. It was the first word that came into his head. It wasn't good at all, but he didn't doubt it. Everyone does, he wanted to add. *Everyone*. That's another reason we have to be very careful who gets in.

'I think that you came here to improve your writing and should do it.' He coughed. 'Otherwise, aren't you wasting your time and money?' He noticed that Lester's small fingers, about the size of his, were flicking the corners of a thick manuscript. 'We all do the same thing,' Ben said. 'We write. It's what we do. What matters most is giving the time and thought to do it well.'

'But I'm interested in writing for money.'

'That's wonderful. There's nothing wrong with that. But for credit – '

Ben raised his finger then leaned across and answered his phone as the intercom buzzed. 'Yes? Put him on.' He motioned toward Lester, one hand cupped over the receiver. 'It's Paul Culver.' His voice changed. 'Just a minute,' he whispered. He saw that Lester hadn't heard of him. 'He has a Pulitzer,' he said. Come on, cheer up. They're still giving them out, he thought.

'Hello. I'm glad you did.' He nodded to Lester. 'I wondered,' he said, 'if you could have lunch the 22nd? Wonderful. I'm hoping you'll want to teach for us.' When he hung up, Lester sat, his eyes on the manuscript he had brought. He didn't look up.

Lester was not impressed.

'I'm sorry,' Ben said, 'I have a meeting in a few minutes. Did you bring something for me to read?' He stood up first.

'No. I'm working on a mystery whenever I have a minute. You haven't answered about soap courses.'

'It's a good idea for non-credit,' Ben said. 'In fact we have a genre conference planned. But we don't offer credit for it.'

'And you won't?'

'I don't think so. You learn it best by doing it.' Ben nodded, standing up. Lester and he were the same height. Lester's tee shirt hung out at his waist.

'Make another appointment for later,' Ben said. 'I'm glad you came.' When Lester was down the hall, he closed the door, then sat back in the chair. He put the file in the wire holder. He looked out the window a moment, collecting his thoughts.

His phone buzzed. 'I have Vice President Pilkington's secretary,' Chuck said.

'Thank you.' Ben pressed the lighted button and began talking. 'Ms Games, could I make a luncheon appointment with Dr Pilkington for next week?' he asked. That would give him at least four days to think things over.

'I'm sorry. He'll be out of town. Is this Mr Escobio?'

'Yes.'

'He's free tomorrow. Is that all right?'

Ben hesitated. 'Yes,' he said nervously.

'I'll check with him and call back if it isn't. At noon you'll come by here?'

'Yes. Thank you.'

Ben hung up.

He left the office immediately and walked down the hall to Danz's office. He went in, saw Frank Danz on the phone and sat down. He wished Danz would hang up. He was always talking to someone. Ben crossed his feet, his shoes lightly polished. He waited three minutes, the second hand of the desk clock hopping from dot to dot. He tried for a minute to listen to the conversation. On the wall were black and white close-ups of ballerinas, conductors, choreographers, a signed photo of Stravinsky. Danz was clarifying everything that he said, patiently.

Finally he hung up and put the gold pen that he took notes with back in his shirt pocket. 'That was Margaret in Art. You can't get her off.'

'Peel wants credit classes taken out of the college,' Ben said.

'I heard it this morning. Who told you?'

'I met with Nona and Daryl.'

'Oh yes. How did that go?' Danz leaned closer, waiting.

A soft rap at the door interrupted them.

'Yes?' Danz called out. 'Come in.' Danz stood up from his desk. 'Is someone there?'

Daryl walked in, carrying a drink in a paper cup. 'Oh Ben,' he said, 'I just went by your office, looking for you. Where's Chuck? Can you and I meet?'

'I can't now,' Ben said.

'At five then, for as long as it takes. I can work late.'

'I'm leaving early.'

'You'll make sure the office is open tomorrow at eight?' Daryl asked. 'I spoke to Sylvia about it already.'

Ben felt like taking off his belt and using it. All right. He meant *enough*. They're my staff. Daryl knew how to make people bark like dogs at him. As if he were a stray in the wrong yard.

Who hired *him?* everyone asked. Nona had. Danz should have had the job.

'I wonder if we shouldn't cut Chuck and hire Sylvia full time,' Daryl said. 'Do we need two in your office?' He held a spiral notebook open in front of him. 'Sylvia doesn't think so.' He wrote down something.

'Chuck's with Mary Oswalt, going over graduating student transcripts.'

'Why?' Daryl asked.

'Our students want to graduate,' Ben said.

'I just want to learn how your office runs so I can help you cut your budget.'

Ben's eyes narrowed and Daryl noticed it.

'We can meet later,' Daryl said. 'Danz, can you come by my office immediately when you're finished?'

'For a few minutes. I have to be in Hollywood this afternoon.'

No one spoke. Daryl sipped the coke, then left. He closed the door slowly, glancing back at them.

Ben looked at Danz, who looked at the door. 'What an asshole,' Danz whispered. 'I wonder what he wants. Keep everything written down,' he said. 'I've got a file of what he's tried to do. If you don't, you'll forget it.'

'They can't squeeze more out of my programme without hurting it.'

'Then they'll hurt it,' Danz said. 'Protect yourself.'

Ben sighed, then stretched, the sun making the cool office drowsy.

'I think I may have something wrong with me,' Danz said. 'My farts smell really bad. They're terrible. I can hardly stand being in the bathroom with myself.' He stacked the loose paper clips on his desk and dropped them into a square plastic container. 'I'm really tired.'

'What could you have?' Ben glanced at his eyes, the tint of his skin. 'How tired are you?'

'I've been waking later and not sleeping well. It's the smell – you can't imagine how bad it is. You know Sara's assistant has mono. Maybe I've got it.'

'No,' Ben said. 'You don't.' He should wash his hands immediately. What had he touched: only the magazine beside him, on the sofa. 'Your eyes aren't yellow.'

'I've already had hepatitis.'

'It's the smog,' Ben said, relieved. He could feel it, too. He could see a cloud of it in the distance, out the window. Like it was being shot off by cannons, towards them. Where it was bad, he couldn't see anything else.

'I should start thinking of getting out of this place.' Danz leaned across to get a cigarette from his coat pocket. 'I've been thinking of business. Maybe stocks.' He leaned back, the collar of his white shirt stiff. He coughed, his face pale in the light.

'Maybe you should see a doctor,' Ben said.

Ben hurried along the brown carpet, down the stairway, the walls grey, through the flimsy door marked 'Men's'. Cigarette butts floated in the drain; water flowed on to the white crystal deodorant. Ben pissed in two streams. It smelled of vitamins.

The toilet in the stall flushed.

He tried to hurry. He glanced up, nodded, then looked down at the porcelain. He thought it was Sara's assistant. The man turned on water in the sink. He began to wash his hands.

'You've got mono?' Ben asked, to be positive. He noticed the striped dress shirt, the expensive haircut, the silk tie.

'That's Kip, Sara's assistant,' the man said. He rubbed his hands vigorously, splattering water. 'I'm getting over amoebic dysentery.' He turned off the faucet, took a paper towel and dried his fingers.

'Oh.' Ben glanced at him again. Who did he work for?

'I'm about over it now. *Never* get it.'

The door opened and closed. Ben shook himself, then zipped up his pants. At the sink he started to turn on the faucet. He took a paper towel, then turned the handle. He avoided the liquid soap. Water ran over his palms, hot. He drew back, took another towel and turned off the faucet. He breathed in deeply outside, in the hall.

As he passed the water fountain close to his office, he looked suspiciously at it, too. Then he opened the door, sat down and began to rub his eyes.

Have I got something? he asked. Could I have mono, too?

He glanced at his watch: 3.15.

That allowed forty-five minutes for traffic. Ben got up and walked to the departmental office. Chuck typed monthly pay vouchers while Sylvia sat on a table and polished her nails purple to match her pants.

'Did you call Howard Israel back?' Chuck asked.

'I will now,' Ben said. In his office he dialled 8, the code, then Howard's number.

'Israel Investments.'

'Is Mr Israel in? Ben Escobio calling.'

'One moment please.'

Ben didn't recognize her voice. She was new and sounded young.

'Ben,' Howard said. 'You got my message?'

'I was going to call anyway.' Ben felt himself relax. He leaned back in his chair, then put his feet on the cluttered desk. 'How's Carolyn?'

'She makes me happy. You sound like you have a cold.'

'I'm just tired. Actually I'm furious with the Dean at this moment.' He hesitated, then added, 'Listen to this, Howard, and tell me what you think. Do you have a minute?'

'Yes, I do. I'm listening.'

Ben began to explain the situation to him.

Half an hour later, he went out the door, locked his office and hurried downstairs.

Over three hundred cars had been stolen on campus the past two semesters. The students had lost hundreds of thousands of dollars' worth of things they owned. One poor coed had been robbed of a seventy-four thousand dollar ring.

Possibly she was the blonde in front of him, her skirt waving hello. She went into the parking garage just as he did. She looked like she could buy a new ring, to match her car.

The high tuition was pocket change.

She closed the door to the Porsche beside his Honda. She didn't look across at him, but gunned the gas pedal then backed, shifted and screamed around the bend to the exit of the parking garage.

Ben backed out slowly, listening for anyone else. At the corner he turned left to the freeway access road.

On the brightly lighted freeway, he went the speed limit. He tried to make himself feel better.

The traffic was grander than a drive-in racing movie, the cars almost colliding, the radios loud, the setting spectacular. He saw the hood ornament of a Rolls, the wide grille, then a '58 Chevy. Next, he noticed a Mercedes convertible pass, a Datsun 280Z, then an Alfa Romeo.

And he was worried about paying the rent.

The radio in his Honda needed repair. It came on, followed by static. He drove with one hand on the selector. The volume was loud.

Ben wished that he could just tell Nona that he would quit.

Another Mercedes passed in the middle lane. Ben glanced across and started to wave. He didn't. He settled back against the seat. He tried to look out from the corner of his eye. The woman was in some series on TV, but he couldn't remember which. He felt embarrassed, thinking he had known her.

She pressed on her gas, her eyes on the road, the packages high on the seat beside her.

Her name was on the tip of his tongue.

He had seen her and whatchamacallit in the past two days.

Stars could pop up anywhere not just in the sky. They ate at delis, pushed carts in grocery stores, drove past and showed up in lines at movies. Nearly everyone he knew either knew one or someone who did. It was like knowing an oil man in Texas or a senator in Washington.

But the city was wrapped up for the stars. The effects of Hollywood made L.A. a lot of what it was: the grandiose architecture, built like movie props, people everywhere dressed to attract attention, enormous housing prices for big salaries, exotic restaurants – all for the beautiful. Didn't everyone in the city want to be gorgeous and show it off?'

Didn't people everywhere? Of course. A little of Hollywood was in every city, but a lot of it was in L.A.

He glanced across, in the next car, just in case. But it was nobody, in an old blue Cadillac.

Their next door neighbour in Odessa, Texas, had had one just like it – only new. The radio static increased and he turned it off. Traffic just ahead slowed. Odessa had oil and high school football and Cadillacs.

At the high school, the football team was called 'Mojo'. No one knew why or what the word meant. But fans at games bellowed 'Mojo – Mojo!' Small children, their parents, and all the students did.

'Mojo!' they shouted with the excitement of 'Help!' or 'Fire!'

He had sat in the stands, wanting to shout it, too.

It meant what they made it. 'Watch out!' 'Win!'

Wasn't that what the sounds that animals made meant?' Animals knew what to make of them.

Moo.

Baa.

Grr.

He spread his lips, grrr vibrated behind his clenched teeth. His breath rose in his throat, grew deep, guttural, then with a hiss, he growled.

Grrr.

Grrrr.

Suddenly he exploded it, rushing out the air 'Woof! Woof!', a bark. That was how a dog really barked. Deep in his throat, a growl, then woof!, an explosion.

Amazing.

He pressed on the gas, then breathed in, growled and barked loudly.

At four, he pulled into the drive on 26th.

What was familiar about Alice was her voice, her hair, her face. He knew how she chose her clothes, what she liked to eat, when she got sleepy. He understood how she learned and what she thought of things. Little thoughts about herself even.

She was the most familiar person in his life.

Her cotton gloves and the red trowel lay on the cement patio. Jules's shovel stuck up from the dirt along the bed of lilies. Her voice came from the backyard. He walked around the house and could see them in front of the garage.

'Daddy!' Jules ran toward him.

Ben loosened his tie. He leaned down to hug him. He tried to understand what Jules was saying.

'Can you snap?' Jules asked. 'Can you?'

'Can I what?'

'Snap,' Jules said.

Ben held up his fingers and snapped them. 'Like that?' He held Jules's hand, to put the fingers into place. 'Press one against the other,' he said, 'then flick them. No. Like this.'

Alice smiled, taking off her gloves. 'How was your day?' she asked.

4

The Movie Screening

'She'd cut me in a second if I block her changes,' Ben said. He believed it. 'I think that Pilkington wouldn't let her though.'

'It doesn't matter what she'd do,' Alice said. 'You shouldn't give in.'

He said nothing, listening. How was he supposed to pay for everything if something happened? He should find a job that made more money.

The coral trees were red-orange along Sunset, then the road narrowed and in the canyon, flowers blossomed on the terraces. Occasionally from the top of a hill, Ben could glimpse the sunset. The smog made it rose coloured. Alice pushed back the visor and looked at her lips in the mirror. She unzipped her purse and put in the kleenex blotted with light pink. 'Oh, Mother called,' she said. 'They're coming Thursday for your birthday. They'll just stay two days.'

Ben shifted into low, then pressed on the brakes before the next curve. The Honda whined. 'I don't want a party,' he said.

'We won't even have cake. Is that all right?'

She knew it wasn't what he wanted. He glanced at his watch: they were still early. He passed the street, shot along cottages to the dark bottom of the canyon, then circled, past a park with swings. The Honda vibrated as it took the hill back to the top, the ocean now on their left. He turned down the street of two-storey houses, the view flowing behind them. He puttered to a stop in front of the long red roof that was even with the road. William and Jess's.

For a moment, he was nervous. Certain houses had prestige

because of who lived in them: the public White House, any governor's mansion, a movie star's place. Most homes of rich business men had prestige according to their cost. The glory was in how much money they exposed and not who lived there. A pantyhose magnate might be surpassed by a toothpaste executive or a sharp stockbroker. Anyone driving by these homes could imagine the inside: conversation pits, TVs the size of refrigerators, bathrooms with bidets, closets like warehouses. But William Bradshaw's house had the prestige that came from his having written important books there. He had worked alone, in his bedroom. His success gave the house a reputation.

The celebrities that entered his doorway and sat in the windowed rooms, the paintings over the fireplace, on the walls, above the entrance, could not resist certain things about him. His fingertips knew the ticklish places under their arms and on the bottoms of their feet. He had a charm in his red socks and polished penny loafers. He could blow it out like smoke rings. He was expert with people because they were what he wrote and cared about.

Ben got out of the car, opened Alice's door and walked along the drive. He stood in the low carport, gazed down at the Mexican roof and beyond at the hills, the flat water, then he pressed the bell.

Who finally knew literature better than oneself? he wondered. Ultimately what anyone thought was right. He knew, deep down. Anyone could speak honestly for themselves if they wanted to. He didn't worry about who was his favourite writer. He gave that prize away in a second, listening to his own feelings. William wrote better than anyone and there was no need to question this point.

There were writers with beautiful novels that he loved. Gorgeous ones. There were others whose books made him worry about the sanity of publishers. There were wonderful, excellent, good, mediocre and terrible novels in every bookstore.

In his world all these books were generally viewed as successes because they were published. He lived in the underworld of manuscripts, where people wanted their novels turned into printed books regardless. But wasn't it better for a bad manuscript to face early rejection rather than scathing or no reviews? Wasn't the frying pan better than the fire? Shouldn't every writer in the world go back over his work once more? Of course, but the quality was usually beside the point. Most that he knew wanted publication more than anything. They underestimated what writing was about.

William was his personal favourite. Ben's opinion created good will between them. Just as if God had given William a beautiful face to look at.

Alice followed him down the steep cement steps to the open door. He knocked, waited, then entered the large room, the wall opposite them glass, the air inside cool from the ocean.

William hurried from the dining room to meet them. He was wearing a coat and tie. His eyes were blue under the clear plastic frame glasses. His hair was short with a slight cowlick. He looked both polite and busy.

'I was just about to make myself a drink,' he said. 'Jess is finishing dressing. What would you like?'

'Scotch,' Ben said. Alice chose wine.

She sat in the centre of the green sofa. Large art books were stacked on the square table in front of them. Ben chose a low chair, then quickly looked about for a new painting. He pointed out a small rectangular one to Alice and listened to William in the kitchen. Ben excused himself, crossed the dining room and walked to the kitchen doorway.

'Can I help?' he asked, and stepped on to the bright white tile.

William was running hot water over an ice tray. He had taken out four glasses, somewhat smudged, Ben noticed. 'I've got it,' William said.

Ben leaned against the counter, looking at photographs on the wall. 'You know the bookstore on Santa Monica, beside the Indian restaurant?' Ben asked.

'I know the man who runs it very well,' William said. 'He handles first editions of my books.' He washed off the cubes of ice and began dropping them into the glasses. 'I don't think he makes much from it.'

'They have special displays of no-frill paperbacks. The books have no author or title. They just have "western" or "mystery" on the cover. They're sixty-five cents. Now you can get a book like a nickel cigar.' Ben watched him generously pour scotch on to the ice. 'Whoever thought of that should be shot.'

'I think I saw them. The man I'm speaking of – ' he handed Ben a glass – 'told me something amusing – ' William picked up Alice's and his drinks and walked into the dining room.

Ben followed him back to the sofa and sat beside Alice. Her gold earrings were glowing next to her long hair.

'I was just telling Ben that I went into a bookstore on Santa Monica Boulevard today and the owner told me he had seen my name on some kind of list. He seemed quite impressed but couldn't recall the book.' William crossed his legs, the red socks brightly contrasting with his slacks. 'I was looking for a new biography of Auden. Then I noticed a book he just might have meant – *The Book of Lists*. Do you know the one I mean?' He started to laugh before he finished. 'There I was under the heading "World's Most Famous Homosexuals". I'm sure he didn't even remember.'

'But he remembered seeing your name,' Ben said.

'Well, exactly. Now tell us how your book is coming,' William said.

'I've got nearly two hundred pages.'

'When can I read them?'

'Pretty soon,' Ben said.

'The sooner the better.'

Ben saw Jess coming down the hallway. His grey sports coat was the silver colour of his short hair. He was very fit.

'We'd better hurry,' Jess said. 'It's a thirty-minute drive.'

Ben stood up first.

'A student of mine told me that he works for an Arab prince,' Ben said, waiting for Alice. 'You can imagine the money the prince has.'

'Yes, I can,' Jess said.

'He was hardly out of my office the other day before I had to stop, shut the door and think quietly to myself. I was too tempted not to. What would I do with that much money? With millions and millions. It was far more interesting to think about that than what I should have been doing.'

'Why would it have to be even that much?' Jess asked.

'Well what would you do with it? With a whole lot just given to you?' Ben asked.

'What would you do?' William asked.

Ben followed them toward the door. 'You know I began to daydream about it, and everything I thought of that I wanted cost money, but not enough. And I'm sure, if I had it, I'd want to do something special or why have so much? I kept changing what I'd buy until what I wanted the money for began to seem silly. If you start comparing what money can buy, you realize that you don't know what you want. The money becomes less important. You're back to what you think about things, and you don't need money for that.' Ben stepped outside and glanced at the deepest blue rising across the ocean, the houses bright on the hills across.

The studio where Jess painted hung like a plum just above them. Jess drew or painted subjects – eye to eye. Step on a scale and get an accurate weight, Ben thought, look at a clock for the right time. Go inside the studio and see how you really look. They walked past the studio up the steps, to the car.

Ben turned up Sunset and down Highway 50 until the Inter-state, then slowed with the traffic.

'Did I tell you that the stars of the picture will be there?' Jess asked. 'There will be a lot of other people, too.'

'It'll be mobbed,' William said.

'I don't think there's been another studio showing. This is the first. Isn't it, William?'

'Yes. I believe so.'

It was Hollywood. The sunglasses the couple were wearing in the next car, in the dark, were Hollywood. So were William and Jess, their own glitter ready. Ben drove through the lighted streets slowly.

'That's Hollywood High,' Jess said as they passed.

Then they were beyond Hollywood and on the freeway to the studio.

'I'll get us wine to drink,' Ben said. Most of the seats in the small theatre were empty, but filling. He leaned up and saw William and Jess talking to a pretty woman on the other side of them. 'Tell them I'm going, OK?'

'Victor Mature is three rows behind us,' Alice whispered.

'We shouldn't look,' Ben said, frowning. He stood up, squeezed past the next couple. 'Excuse me.' He couldn't help glancing back to see if Alice was right. Yes. It looked like him. Ben continued, knocking against the man's knees at the end of the aisle.

'Excuse me.' The man pressed his legs to one side and Ben hurried by. He went up the red-carpeted aisle. The reception area was a hallway leading to studio offices. Folding tables with white cloths and bowls of wine were being set up. Ben stood at the end of the line. Everyone around him had his attention. The line didn't budge; the waiter wasn't quite ready to serve. Ben looked at his watch. He could smell sweet lilac perfume on the person behind him.

Near the door a thick, moustached man in his twenties, wearing tight faded jeans and a blue silk shirt had the full attention of people around him. He's got to be somebody, Ben thought. The man had a short beard of fuzzy black hair. He rolled his eyes, smoking. Ben took an instant dislike to him.

He wore a gold necklace with turquoise stones in the medallions.

As Ben took Alice's and his wine and went back down the aisle, the small auditorium had filled.

In his seat, Ben loosened his striped tie and sipped the wine.

'George Peppard is to your left, six rows down,' Alice said.

He hesitated, looked, then re-counted rows. Was that George Peppard? 'He looks fat.'

'I know it's him.' Alice touched Jess's sleeve and whispered. Jess nodded.

'I told you.'

'But he's overweight. And he's wearing glasses.'

'Well, give him a break,' Jess whispered, looking toward them. 'How are you going to look at fifty?'

'Is he fifty?' Ben asked.

'I think that's Steven Spielberg on the first row,' she said. 'Isn't it, Jess?'

'Yes it is.'

'Don't point,' Ben said.

'I'm still like that, too,' Jess said. 'I still gawk.'

'Don't look at them,' Ben said to Alice.

'I'm not,' she said.

Obviously she was. Ben thought that she acted ten years old. His watch must be fast, he decided. Or the showing was late. He searched the faces in front of him for someone else he recognized. Suddenly a woman with vivid blonde hair turned around. 'There's Stephanie Powers on the end of the row in front of us.'

'It is,' Alice said. 'And – '

'Shhh,' he said.

He moved his leg back so that the woman coming down the aisle could take the seat beside him. The seat creaked when the heavy man with her sat down. Ben could smell strong perfume and noticed her red hair to her bare shoulders. In an instant, he caught an eyeful. Look who she is, he wanted to say. Was it true? Alice was absorbed in the credits. Then the screen glowed with the redhead's name. And her face was fifty feet wide. Ben moved his hand quickly off the arm-rest and nudged Alice with his finger.

'What?' Alice said.

In the audience, he thought that she could have been using a megaphone. Then he saw that Arlene Ball was looking directly at him. One second later she turned to the screen.

'That's Arlene Ball,' Alice said. 'She's starring in this movie.'

He sat back, blinders on his eyes, the screen photographing Paris.

Let's all go, he thought. Yves Montand began to sing. The two of them were dancing at a wedding, the sun against her red hair like fire. On the screen her face didn't have a wrinkle. Her large eyes made his glad, and her wide, almost oval mouth was red. He liked her nose, the smile. He glanced uneasily at the next seat.

She was kind of pretty, but her hair was wrong. It shouldn't have been behind her ears or fuzzy. He could see freckles all over her forehead, maybe because she'd been in the sun. And she wore long earrings with green balls the size of olives. Alice was much more beautiful.

On the screen someone was shooting at Montand. The gunman had hidden in the flowers and come out boldly, firing.

It was unbelievable and she was awful in this, her mouth twisted. She must have been mad at the script, he thought.

He could see her clearly beside him. She had put on half glasses that made her look like a psychiatrist, and she studied the screen.

Ben could see her hand tightening on a kleenex in her fist. He looked safely at her face which was absorbed with the screen. On the screen she was one of the most beautiful women in the world. She had found her place. Wasn't she lucky that everyone could see her magic? In person she looked plain.

The lights finally came on, with applause. Everyone must be glad it's over, he thought. He heard people complimenting her at once, like a babbling brook.

He leaned across. 'I liked it very much,' he said.

She held her expression, one moment. 'Thank you,' she said.

He stood in the foyer with another glass of wine that had a hole in it. Then he drank Alice's too and agreed that yes, she should call the babysitter. William had seen a telephone by the entrance and showed her. White deli sandwiches, fancy dips and a display of cut-up vegetables and fruits had been brought in and placed on two more tables covered with white cloths.

'Excuse me,' Ben said, and slipped from the circle talking to them. He wanted more wine and stood, sipping it. The white wine was cold and wet.

The man Ben had spotted at the door walked up, holding a drink. He was the producer.

Ben didn't think he could be thirty. Yet the film had cost eighteen million dollars. His last film had grossed over eighty million. He was a genius, people said.

'I'm Ben Escobio,' he said, quickly.

The producer said nothing but nodded. He smiled, looking embarrassed and waited for Ben to say something else.

'I enjoyed the film.'

'Thank you.'

'I really did enjoy it,' Ben said.

'I believed you the first time.' His dark eyes screwed up, closely. 'You mean you didn't, or you wouldn't have repeated it.'

'Not at all.'

The producer obviously knew, but he was back to listening and not speaking. He waited several seconds, flattening his long moustache with his little finger.

You're right, Ben thought. It embarrassed him.

'How long are you staying in Los Angeles?' the producer asked.

'I live here. We moved from Atlanta two years ago.'

He nodded, obviously hearing him, then he turned, toward someone who tapped him on the shoulder.

Ben finished the wine and held the clear empty cup. He rubbed his fingernail along the side of it, the ice making the side haze over. He stood a moment, wondering what to say. Then he noticed David Goldman not three feet from him, waving.

Ben walked across and stopped beside him, like he stood under the shade of a tree. Another writer. A good one. He understood writers. They had a kind of honesty about them. They expected each other to be interesting, not perfect. In private they could take the most glorious moments – the acceptance of an Academy Award, the opening of a Broadway play – and get it in focus, making it life-size.

'You look tired,' David said.

'Well I am,' Ben said. He wished he could reach across, turn out the light switch, and put his head down on a pillow.

'I finished your book,' Ben said. 'I liked it very much.'

'It's small,' David said. 'I haven't found anyone to publish it.'

'But it's wonderful. You know that.'

'I liked it,' he said. He took his drink in a gulp. Up close, his eyebrows were like weeds. 'I wrote it when I was in trouble out here,' he said. 'I escaped from Los Angeles by thinking about it.'

'It really is good,' Ben said. 'Something will happen with it.' He could have put it on a list in a minute for everyone to see. It was quiet, and wonderful. The careful people inside had voices that he knew. 'I really did,' he said.

'My mother likes it the best of all my books,' David said.

You have to tell a writer over and over, Ben thought. It's one of his good points. 'Why don't we have lunch Friday?'

'That's fine. I'm free at noon.' David motioned toward someone behind Ben. 'Have you met Arlene?' he asked suddenly. He hugged, his arms wide, then kissed her, his lips smacking. He introduced Ben.

Standing up, she was thinner. Ben could remember her taking off her clothes in her old movies, her shiny face, the lipstick bright. If she had done it at that moment, she would have been pale, fragrant, her eyes avoiding the camera.

'Hello,' she said.

He couldn't tell if she remembered they had sat by each other.

He had seen her in movies where people had waited blocks to get in the theatre. They had never been disappointed. He had loved her films. They were worth a lot to him. He wanted to tell her. He had known her for years. Hers wasn't just a job. She was a star.

He looked closer at her eyes.

He wanted her to be wonderful. Like it wasn't just acting or talent, but it was her character that was so good. As if she really were all the roles she portrayed.

'I've been on the set all day,' she said. She leaned down, massaging one of her calves. 'Did you like the picture?' She looked at David.

'I did,' he said. 'I always love you.'

She looked at Ben.

'I did too,' he said.

She took another sip from her cup. She shrugged. 'It needs more editing. There's a writer in Wisconsin who has written a play just for me. I'm going to do it next. It's lovely, David. It's about an ageing star who meets an old lover and starts over. Would you read it for me sometime?'

'Yes I would. Could I get you another drink?'

'No. On Sunday I'm doing *Love Boat in Honolulu*.' She set down her cup on a table. 'I'm trying to leave without anyone noticing because I still live in the Valley. I have a 6 a.m. call in Malibu.'

'Walk out with me,' he said. 'No one will know you're going.'

'Would you?' she asked.

Ben hesitated a second before telling her how much he had liked the film. Wait a minute, he thought. But she was gone. He saw her turn, not looking at anyone. Another second she and David were at the door. He saw it open, people beside it standing back.

He got another cup of wine. Then one for David and waited. He suddenly wanted to see her films again. He knew that they would be different now.

The car hurried on its own along Hollywood Boulevard in the dark. Everyone was out, just as they were. He finally had drunk the right amount and his worries had blown out the window a few blocks from the studio. People on the streets were more exciting than the store windows. Hookers in miniskirts, boys without shirts, and whoever had something to sell tried to show it. Especially in their faces. Selling things at night was completely different from in the daytime. The traffic ahead continued. Ben looked up at Vine and tried to spot David's office. He didn't have time to count the floors. He stopped at a light.

The Howard Johnson's on the corner had customers. A block to the right, Decca Studios was shaped like a stack of records, lighted, the parking lot below. Across the street a woman shopped in a store window of Fredericks. Her wig was black, curly, the red material of her thin dress accentuating her hips. He wondered what exactly she noticed in the window. She moved away quickly when a man walked up and stood beside her.

Ben pressed on the gas. The TicToc restaurant on their left had closed for the night.

He felt that being in the car with Jess and William and Alice was a place too. Just like Hollywood and Vine Streets were. He was glad to be where he was at that moment.

Ben opened his mouth and spoke, quickly. 'There's something beautiful about being anywhere,' he said, 'but look at where we are.' At the top of the hill, the lights below were like a horn. Office buildings and houses were set in the dark hills. He drove slowly because he was drunk. Alice scooted closer to him. The wind from the open window blew against her hair.

'William,' he said, 'tell us a secret. Something you've never told anyone.' He was prepared to ask again.

'Well, what about?' William hesitated. No one else spoke. 'I can't think of anything I haven't told anyone.' He began to laugh.

'I can,' Jess said. 'But isn't that why it's a secret?'

'Then let me ask you questions,' Ben said.

'All right.'

He pressed on the gas, just as the light turned.

'What would you write now if you had never written a word?' he asked. 'Would it be about Paris?' Ben asked.

'Who gives a damn about Paris!'

'Well, what would you write?'

'Oh, I don't know. About my life now I suppose.'

Ask him what only he can tell you. That's what we're for. To know about our own lives, Ben thought.

For a second, Ben glanced at Alice. He wondered what on earth she was doing in the car. Were they like a pair of eyes?

'Uh oh,' Ben said, 'there's a policeman behind us.'

The blue light flashed inside the Honda. No one spoke while he drove with perfect concentration until the white car passed, its bubble light circling. Ben sighed, relieved. Then he thought of work. In the morning, couldn't he shower and go back to work and let the job be a pleasure? Would Nona and Daryl let him alone?

'Look,' he said, pointing toward the valley. The San Diego freeway was as beautiful as a line of fireflies. The movie stars were shadows behind, and in the distance, there was a rosy hue of lights.

5

Housework

Alice opened her eyes, the pillows comfortable, the carved headboard nearly to the height of the windows. They had oiled rather than varnished it. The wardrobe across the room had a narrow mirror that needed resilvering. She had polished the light applewood. She glanced at the small clock on the bed table. Five o'clock. They had bought the Japanese screen behind the bureau at an auction in Omaha and carried it blocks in the snow to their apartment. It wouldn't fit in a cab. The new wallpaper in that highrise had been light blue and green, and outside the window, Omaha had stayed white with snow. The figurine on top of the bureau was one of the first things they had bought in Mississippi; its gilt around the porcelain base was still dark, with light blue and violet painted on the clothes.

She was as used to handling Ben's worries as her own. They would have been much easier for her to list because he repeated them like a rosary. He asked about them as if he were picking out something to buy. What did she think of this worry or that one? When she ventured an opinion, he worried about whatever side she didn't take. Was she sure? He almost never worried about anything that she couldn't tolerate. He worried about different things from her.

She wouldn't agree that he was fat, but she listened to his plans for dieting and saw that his slacks were too tight. So were hers. She understood the pressures that his job created. She knew the people that he talked about from work, through his eyes. She didn't care that he didn't listen when she complained about keeping house. His expression when she tried to, made her feel angry, though. He worried about money enough never to look at a bill that came in the mail.

She genuinely disliked his insistence on worrying about what had already happened in their past. It didn't matter what – everything they had ever done – should they have gone to the University of Massachusetts or have quit good jobs in New York or teaching in Florida. Should he have written an entirely different book rather than the last one he did? Would another subject have been better? When he worried about their life together, he began to criticize. What they had wanted then didn't matter. Had they made a mistake, he wondered.

If she thought about it that way, as she did now, in bed, the windows open and the blankets over them, she felt that his unhappiness was her fault. She knew he didn't think so; he could criticize himself and her as if it weren't personal. As if he were talking about someone passing by who would never know what he said.

She understood why he worried about Nona. She worried, too.

She cared a lot about his job.

Alice turned over and pulled on the blanket to get some from under Ben. She yawned, closed her eyes, opened them, then slipped from the bed and went into the bathroom. Light from the two windows was soft on the white bathroom fixtures. She sat on the commode and felt chilly. She saw that the door shutting in the dirty clothes had come open. She hadn't had time to do the wash. She would before they woke. And finish the dishes that she had left. She remembered that she had to press his blue shirt. She rubbed her eyes, then yawned, covering her mouth. She could feel the wine that she had drunk.

It's Ben's birthday, she remembered. She returned to the bedroom, got back in bed and kissed him. She sat up.

She remembered that when she and Ben were in high school,

one night she had cried because he had told her that he didn't want children. She had wanted four or five, but she had given in. Now, with Jules in bed in the next room, she thought of how Ben loved him.

At six a.m., the luminous minute hand of the clock circled in the dark. Ben slipped from the warm blankets, taking the yellow one at the foot. He left Alice sleeping. He turned on the light in the living room, got his notebook from the desk, then lay against the green striped sofa pillow. He rubbed his cold feet together.

Dale Smith was finishing his sixth novel and a screenplay, he had said over the phone. There were certain writers in his department whose works were reported on like the weather. Another book was coming. Get ready.

Everyone would talk about it.

He pulled the blanket over him and picked up the ballpoint pen. Then he turned and looked back toward the kitchen door. As she hurried to him, Snowy's paws tapped against the linoleum. She walked across the orange carpet in the dining room to the sofa, her long tail wagging. She tried to lick him in the face. Her pink gums, underneath the furry beard, were parted on one side like she would laugh.

'Good girl.' He stroked his fingers along her backbone. Her teeth were yellow and shiny. She opened her mouth, making a high squeal. 'Yes,' he said. Her eyes met his. She squealed again, then pressed her nose against his arm. Her lips spread, the pink bright. She whined.

'Hello,' he said. 'How are you this morning?'

She whined again, then put both front paws on the sofa cushion. She licked his arm with her tongue.

Sometimes he thought that she might talk.

Ben leaned down and stroked the black and white fur on her neck. 'Say something,' he said. 'Go ahead. One word.'

She looked directly into his eyes.

126

Wouldn't a word from her be more important than a whole literary career?

He petted her thin fur. She wagged her tail and made the rabies medal around her neck jingle. She began to lick his fingers.

One word could be so important in the right place.

'Sit, girl.' He wiped off the saliva on to the blanket. He turned back to the paper and closed his eyes. He had to think about his novel. A million words.

At eight, he put the notebook back into the centre drawer of the desk. He took a deep breath and shut the drawer. He hurried to the wilted roses in the blue vase on the mantel. They had bothered him the whole time he wrote. He stopped to pull the colourful petals from their centres until he had a handful of red, yellow ones, light pink, orange. Their smell was fragrant in his palms.

He carried the petals into the hallway, spilling several on to the carpet, and went through the open bathroom door. Water ran furiously, filling the old porcelain tub. He dropped the petals into the water. They swirled, madcapping by the spigot. 'Move back,' he said to Jules. Then he took off his underwear and sat naked in the cold water, the petals a delight, Jules laughing.

Ben soaped his face, arms and chest. He washed his hair and leaned his scalp under the faucet to rinse it. The petals flattened; many of them tore apart along their frail veins. Jules played behind him, sticking them to his back and to the sides of the tub.

'Ben, it's 8.30.' Alice brought the spatula that she used to turn bacon into the bathroom with her. 'Happy birthday! Jules, it's Daddy's birthday.'

'I'm hurrying,' Ben said.

'Don't forget my parents are coming.' She laid down the spatula and began to comb back her hair, slipping a rubber band around it. 'I'm glad you're seeing Pilkington.' She looked away from the mirror and toward him.

Ben noticed her face, her thin waist. He pinched the bulge around his navel.

Alice smoothed on lipstick, then picked up the spatula. 'You'd better hurry.' She bent down, pushing petals back into the tub. He saw how many of them had fallen off on to the floor.

The house they rented could be bought for three hundred thousand dollars cash. Outside of California it would have sold for sixty thousand. The rent was a thousand a month and the inside needed paint. The traffic on 26th was noisy in their bedroom at three in the morning when the nearby bars closed. They had been robbed twice in one year.

He rubbed soap on to his fingers, thinking. He began to shave, dipping the razor in the water. A yellow plastic duck floated by. He soaped his face and turned on the hot spigot. He would have to go over their budget again. Then he frowned, thinking of what to say to Pilkington.

In the bedroom, Ben flicked the light switch, crossed the room and pulled on the carved handles of the rosewood chest. He couldn't find underwear in the drawer with the brown and blue rolled up socks. He tugged at the top drawer, then noticed that Alice had laid his shorts, along with a pressed shirt, on the bed. He chose the blue tie with a narrow maroon stripe and wrapped it under the collar before he buttoned the sleeves.

After looking in the mirror, he hurried into the kitchen where Alice was cooking breakfast.

He opened the refrigerator door, to get out the carton of orange juice.

'Happy birthday,' Alice said again.

Ben nodded and smiled.

'I'm making a low calorie cake. OK?'

He nodded again. Irritated. He would go off his diet. The

refrigerator light blinked, then dimmed. Ben held the door open wider, and looked behind the half gallon of milk.

Alice blew him a kiss.

'Can we wait until tonight for birthdays?' he asked.

'Do you want bacon and eggs?' Alice laid strips on to the skillet, the burner hot.

'No.' He did not. Bacon was going to kill all of them. He moved the milk, noticing the small print on the blue top. Just as he had expected – whole milk – the low fat carton had a purple top. He raised the lid of a cold pyrex dish next on the shelf. The moment he did, he remembered the carrots inside, the sauce congealed. They were at least – he tried to think – two weeks old. Behind it, a smaller dish was turned longways. He took it out, too. Alice's mother's refrigerator was populated with little covered dishes of scraps she served as leftovers until every dab was swallowed. That was bad enough. But Alice saved them for weeks, like a scientific experiment, until they were no longer part of any meal that he remembered and had to be gotten rid of immediately, the instant they were found.

Ben emptied green beans from one dish into the trash, a little mould like hair on top of the skins. He squatted and peered farther back on the bottom shelf.

'I'm going to clean out the refrigerator this morning,' Alice said in a peculiar tone of voice.

'We shouldn't keep leftovers.' Ben said.

The next dish had roast beef that had dried, yet changed colour. Ben turned on the faucet and soaked then squeezed a dishrag to wipe off the glass shelf above the vegetable bin. He rubbed, scraping his fingernail over a decomposed piece of dark lettuce. It looked like carbon.

Alice was busy at the stove. She began to hum like he wasn't there.

He thought that if she would just admit that she didn't like to clean, he wouldn't complain. Why, who did like it?

Instead, Alice acted as if the kitchen were clean. It was a

dare – anything but agreeing with her was being critical. Look how dirty this is, he thought. Why isn't it a subject for conversation?

Ben wiped the rag across the shelf then frowned at a glob of ketchup hardened in the corner of the shelf. He ran the rag over it, smearing red. In the middle was a white cap to a ketchup bottle. He got up, went to the sink and rinsed the rag. Then he remembered the moment that he himself had dropped the bottle cap and left it. He hated screwing them back on, and had meant to pick it up later. He stretched his fingers back toward the corner. Then he put the rag in the sink and shut the refrigerator. He turned off the faucet.

She stirred biscuit mix in a bowl and had just buttered the aluminium tray to cook them in. 'What do you want for tonight?' she asked.

He wanted little gourmet dinners with broiled tomatoes and steaming white fish served on candlelit tablecloths with soft music. Couldn't he do that, if it were his responsibility? He thought so. Hordes of women would laugh at this, he knew. He wanted the house, the meals, and their schedules set in logical order.

He looked across at the clothes stacked on top of the washer. She boiled the clothes, as if they were going to eat them. It was a survival of the fittest, with his shirts looking worn out and frightened the first time she washed them.

Ben watched her turn the bacon, then set the fork on the stove top.

Use a paper towel, he wanted to say.

In twenty years of marriage she had not listened to a word he had said about cleaning. His mention of it affected her physically. He was welcomed in the kitchen like a Japanese bomber at Pearl Harbor. There would be no change. She did not give in. She was as passive and as strong as air.

His tactic was temporarily to insist on things his way. But they would change back. She would have hers any moment that he let up. He stepped over to the stove, broke off the end of a piece of bacon and chewed.

'The biscuits will be ready in five minutes,' she said, setting the tray into the hot oven.

They smelled delicious. He decided that he would eat one and cut back on calories at lunch. 'I'll have one,' he said.

Alice cracked the white eggs on the rim of the pan, dropped them into the hot grease, and put the shells into a bowl.

Suddenly the pipes at the side of the house began to whine loudly.

'Is that Jules?' she asked. She went to the window over the sink, leaned closer, then called out: 'Jules, have you got the water on? Don't get your clothes wet.' She hesitated. 'Turn it off.' She picked up the dishrag and put it over the faucet to dry.

'You'll feel better after your meeting with Pilkington,' she said.

He nodded, saying nothing. He immediately wanted to say how he was sure it was wrong. It wasn't really, but it *could* be.

'You shouldn't worry so much,' she said.

'I don't think I have a choice,' he said. He straightened his tie, then walked on to the porch. 'Come on, honey,' he said, 'look at Jules.'

Don't go the freeway, Ben suggested to himself. But at Wilshire he glanced at his watch, told himself he had to, crossed the overpass and entered the traffic. He pressed down on the gas pedal, changing into the freeway centre lane. The number of cars increased as he passed the Santa Monica city limit. The cars were steaming, their exhaust a mirror. Just ahead they began to slow; he shifted gears. He touched the brake, pressed in on the clutch. In a moment he had to stop. He glanced in the back seat to make sure his jacket wasn't getting wrinkled. He wished he didn't have to commute.

He sat, hands on the wheel. He should write Tom about reviewing more books. It wasn't much, but $100 counted.

Several cars ahead, traffic began to move. He let out on the clutch, the tyres slowly rolling. The banks along the freeway were paved. The cars billowed, his window down and his elbow resting on the door. Oh come on. Hurry. Cars were lined in both directions as far as he could see. He signalled, then changed to the right lane. At the Bundy exit, he turned off the freeway. He would go Pico.

He passed Setco, the glass office building with his dentist, then a vacant lot. He turned right on Pico Boulevard. To hell with the freeway.

Across the street, green and yellow striped curtains covered the display of an aquarium supply. He let out on the clutch, then pressed on the gas. He crossed Princeton, the post office on his right. He saw a Jewish bakery with Yiddish signs, a coffee shop with a striped awning. Suddenly he was in a neighbourhood of flowers and well-kept lawns. The blocks were eyefuls, changing as Los Angeles did. Past the Jewish neighbourhood, the two-storey stucco houses began to disappear. The street became crowded with small shops and colourful signs, many Spanish. The cars alongside him grew old, their exhaust coughing, loud music spilling from the open windows.

He passed a row of stores he didn't care about, then spotted a foreign grocery. A large furniture business, its windows plyboarded, and a theatre with billboards in Korean were next. He stopped on red.

He tried to hold his breath behind a '58 Chevrolet that from all the fumes could have been on fire. A Spanish girl sat in the front seat. A few feet north of where he sat, and he would be in her car sitting beside her. Talking about personal things in her life – her job, what she wanted to buy, her boyfriend. He didn't think that she was married. She was listening to music on the radio. He looked out at the store fronts. If his life were two or three feet to the right, he would be on the sidewalk, looking out of work like everybody else and ignoring the traffic. He stared a second too long at a man in a shiny blue shirt who was drinking out of a half pint. The man looked back unhappily.

One inch in any direction could start his life over, throw him from the car, change his job, his clothes, his face. How could anyone ever be bored? Just turn a corner. Open an eye. Budge. Everything had its angle. It changed.

It was fragile.

He flipped on the radio. He pressed the button for Spanish music. Wasn't it true, though? The plethora of other people around him was like a dream. They made Los Angeles cloudy with smog, anxious with violence. He stopped, missing another light.

He couldn't help feeling good. He was curious about everyone. People were too much alike for him not to care for them and yet every detail of them was different. There was someone else – in the Plymouth signalling right. For a second Ben turned, too. Through the rear-view mirror, he saw an older couple behind him. Ben kissed, his lips pooched. He could not resist. He wanted to know the man driving the Plymouth, the couple, the man staring back at him from the curb. Everyone. *Think of it*. People in Idaho, New York, Texas, Canada, France, China, Africa, Iceland. The world was filled with them. And he took it for granted.

If he didn't know them, *who* were they?

Who are *you*? he asked himself.

Everything mattered. He did, Alice, Jules, the cars, the stores, every second of life. His had already started. Time was going fast.

Let's go, he thought, the light still red.

He sat in the Honda, flushed. These things are here, he thought, in my life.

I didn't ask for them.

6

Counting on People

Eleven o'clock. Ben rapped against the door-frame, the door open to Daryl's office.

'Morning,' Daryl said, looking up and pushing back his chair from his desk.

Well, let's be friendly then. Ben entered and sat on the upholstered chair. He stretched out his arms. His dislike of Daryl wasn't personal. He thought it was important for Daryl to do his job well. But Daryl shouldn't try to bully. Wasn't a supervisor's job like a farmer's? To help things grow? To nourish? Not to shield sunlight from what was thriving.

Daryl grinned even wider, then picked up the receiver to call Corrine, his assistant. 'Would you like coffee?' he asked. 'I believe she has hot tea, too.'

'No thanks,' Ben said.

'This meeting could take us through lunch.'

'I have a luncheon appointment. You said it would be half an hour.'

'Oh.' Daryl shook his head in a series of small nods. He hung up. 'I'm going to work evenings on Thursdays,' he said. 'I'll be evaluating classes for the Dean. I want to schedule evaluations of your teachers particularly.'

Ben immediately glanced outside the window and noticed a car pull past, turning through the brick gates toward the centre of campus. 'You want to evaluate teachers in my programme?' he asked.

'Yes. We will have to cut back.'

Ben turned to face him. 'You know that already? And you decide?'

Daryl's smile grew more obvious.

'I don't think we need evaluations in graduate education,' Ben said. 'That's done in the hiring process. Our job is to help faculty in every way we can.' He tried to look calm. 'You know the qualifications of our teachers. They're all very successful writers themseves. Read their books. They don't have to teach. What they do teach couldn't easily be evaluated by someone who isn't a writer.'

'I disagree,' Daryl said quickly. 'I'm experienced in evaluating teachers no matter what their subject is. That's one of my specialties.'

'Good. I appreciate differences in pedagogical ideas,' Ben said. 'And we differ. I won't have you going into my classes. The teachers would quit. I promise you.'

'Oh I don't think so.'

'I would think you have other things to do.'

'We'll put it on the calendar to discuss later.' Daryl cleared his throat, hesitating.

Ben scooted back the chair.

'I have this printing invoice,' Daryl said. 'For $865. What's it for?'

'We've met about that already.'

'There's no information with the invoice.'

'It's for printing 5,000 brochures.'

'I know. But what is the breakdown? How much did the colour cost? The folding?'

'We have a hundred thousand dollar profit in my programme. I don't think $865 is high.'

'I don't know,' Daryl said. 'It could be.'

'Then don't sign it. We won't have a brochure.'

Daryl took the ballpoint from his pocket and co-signed the voucher. 'You shouldn't get so upset when I ask you something.'

Ben leaned closer. He began to read the memo Daryl was drafting on a yellow tablet. The desk was cleared, otherwise. The words meant nothing. He didn't look up.

'I think you're doing an excellent job,' Daryl said.

Ben stood up. He saw that it was nearly 11.30 on the desk clock.

'Sure you won't have lunch?' Daryl asked. 'I have time.'

'I have an appointment,' Ben said. He walked out, shut the door and nodded to Corrine, Daryl's assistant. He hurried down the black rubber runner to his office. He closed the door, told Chuck he was leaving and went down the outside steps to the brick and ivy path leading to the Vice President's office.

The degrees after his name were as valuable as owning rare stamps. B.A., M.A., Ph.D., LL.D., M.D., Ph.B . . . It was unlikely for anyone to use all the training except for the pursuit of knowledge. Scholar. Scientist. University Vice President. The degrees indicated that Pilkington loved universities, was exceptionally bright, and something more than educated. But what? Ben waited in the quiet outer office. He thumbed nervously through a shiny alumni journal that listed the university's top administration. Pilkington was everyone's superior.

Ben listened to the secretary handle the telephone efficiently. 'He's off now,' she said suddenly. 'I'll tell him you're here.'

Ben watched her punch the intercom button. He laid down the magazine, straightened his tan and white tie, the toes of his oxfords just shiny, not too much.

The Vice President came out of his office a moment later, in a good mood. Ben could tell. His eyes were dark brown, his hair wiry and his bushy eyebrows black, blending into his skin. 'Ready?' He stuck his arms through his plaid sports coat, then straightened it across his shoulders. 'I was in my lab until eleven. I'm afraid it's made me a bit late.' He glanced at his watch. 'Not much though.'

Ben hurried to open the door. 'Where's your lab?' He followed, leaving the bright offices, going into the empty hallway and toward the stairs. The red painted cement floor was the rich colour of terracotta.

'Hidden. I have a surprisingly complete one in the basement of Garwood. I'll show you sometime if you like.'

'What are you researching?'

'I warn you – don't get me started.' He hesitated, waving as they passed someone in a pinstriped suit. 'People tell me I get carried away.'

'What is it? I am interested.' Ben glanced at the glittering letters above the President's office.

'It's quite interesting really. You're sure I haven't told you?'

'No.'

'Well,' Pilkington said, his voice deep, 'you know that most anthropologists pinpoint Africa as having the progenitor for man. I'm sure you were told that in school. And obviously so, for Africa has been searched with the greatest degree of accuracy. But why should you assume that?' Pilkington hesitated long enough for Ben to look up.

Ben started to think quick about an answer.

'I don't. A number of my colleagues in the field would disagree with me on this and many of my views.' He took long steps that Ben matched as they started down the stairs. 'I'd be worried if what I wrote wasn't questioned. Wouldn't you?'

Ben nodded, to please him.

'I disagree strongly with assuming things. And my research – as that of others – indicates that many of our assumptions have been wrong. Are you aware of the Won Tonu find?' At the entrance, Pilkington opened the door. A circular flowerbed of blooms was shaded by eucalyptus. 'I actually have pieces of it in my lab, on loan from a colleague at the University of Huang. Of course everything is preliminary and only the two of us have examined them. But the questions that they raise would amaze you. These I have tested out at five million years.'

'Really?'

'Yes. And it's likely that man-like creatures were alive along with Australopithecus. This is why I say you were told wrong in school. Not wrong – but scientists have had to update their views. We have to see several lines of human genera as parallel to human lineages. There is no missing link that I know of.'

Ben had always wondered how to pronounce Australopithecus. He realized he had said it wrong for over a decade. But not many times. 'How *do* you date something?' he asked. All he could remember from his one anthropology class was the teacher's face lecturing on the sex life of baboons. Schwartz had looked like one, and Ben had taken this as evidence of evolution.

'Well, you can date fossils and geological layers where they're found.' Pilkington shook his long index finger. His voice rose. 'There are two basic approaches.' He stopped walking, but continued to talk. 'One depends on comparing layers of earth at various sites. You can use nitrogen or fluoride. Or you might consider geomagnetic changes in rocks to date them.' The wind puffed at his hair and blew against the hem of his coat. 'Another way is to measure changes in geological materials – such as the decay of radio isotopes or fission track studies. There are a number of ways. But certainly dates that we all used to take for granted are known to be wrong. Dating includes error. Are we going to the faculty club?'

'I thought we would,' Ben said. 'Or there's Ambrose.'

'Then let's go to Ambrose.' Pilkington turned between the stucco building and the large new arts centre. He caught Ben's eye.

'What was five million years ago like?' Ben asked quickly.

'Of course no one knows. Skeletons give us some information. We know things for sure that we didn't before because we aren't limited to our eyes.'

Ben listened, ignoring the glances of students as they passed. This man, he wanted to tell them, is the academic head of this university. He should be exact, learned, enthusiastic. Well, he actually is.

'Some contemporaries believe that human-like characteristics of fossils mean that animals did human-like things. And our views about the Ramapithecene are undergoing changes. At first we thought of these as leading to human evolution, but new information shows that speculation about their using tools isn't justified.'

'Oh,' Ben said, trying to follow. He began to watch Pilkington's nose. It was very shiny with sunlight on it.

'There are limits, to what we can learn about fossils. With something that's living, you can go from behaviour to biomechanics, to detailed analysis of muscles, bones and joints. But with fossils you can go only from the structure of bones to projected physical behaviour.'

The words were like fireflies, with Ben running after them. Wait, he thought. One minute. This one is lovely. Then another lit up. He truly knew nothing about it and would like to learn.

'I'm running on,' Pilkington said. 'I warned you – '

'But don't you have an M.D.? Were you a medical doctor?'

'Yes,' Pilkington said. 'But I only practised a while.'

They began to walk along a narrow path planted with monkey grass. They passed the union and Ben saw Ambrose Hall.

'I've been looking forward to meeting with you again. I'm glad you're Vice President,' Ben said.

'So am I. And I'm glad you're glad.'

'But how do you have time to do research?' Ben asked.

'How could I not? Just last night I was at a party where a board member of our university expressed concern about holding graduate courses with less than five. I told him about the famous class that Professor Edwin Honig held in nuclear physics at Berkeley. Have you heard of it?'

Ben shook his head.

'Three students were enrolled – which would be reason enough to have cancelled it at most state universities. But all three students were eventually to win the Nobel prize. Would you say that that physics class should have been cancelled for lack of students?'

'That's wonderful,' Ben said.

'A major research institution can't afford not to provide time for its faculty and administration and students. I've been putting down my ideas about this. Of course mine is scientific writing – crass stuff, not like yours.'

'I'd like to read it,' Ben said. 'I'm sure it isn't crass.'

'I thought all scientific writing was,' Pilkington said. He opened the glass door and the air conditioning was cold. Inside, the red velvet tie to the brass rail was undone. There was no line. Ben could see several vacant tables. They were lucky. The salad buffet was set up in front of them.

The waiter led them to a table by the window and left the big red menus.

'Would you like a glass of wine?' Ben asked.

'I believe I would. If you do.'

Ben spotted the steward and ordered. Then he looked past Pilkington at the busy tables. Ben leaned closer, his voice lower. 'I could tell you certain things about my programme in the past that would startle you. They're not true now.'

'I could tell you stories that you wouldn't believe about other programmes. Then and now. What area are you talking about?'

'Things that used to be done that caused certain other chairmen not to support us. We needed changes. A student came into my office about a month ago,' Ben continued, choosing an extreme example. 'He asked if I would be his thesis director. We spoke a few mintues and I decided that I wouldn't, but I asked my assistant to check the student's records. He had dropped out of school two years before.'

Pilkington was listening carefully.

'When my assistant brought the file, she asked if we could talk privately. I said yes and stepped outside with her. It seems that the student had registered for thesis once – a project he began and dropped – and the professor gave him an A. He gave him an A, yet the student had turned in nothing. The student had completed all other course requirements and filed for graduation, contingent on the approval of his thesis. When the registrar's office got the grade, the student was graduated.' Ben saw how shocked Pilkington was. 'I told him I would be his thesis director and am working with him on his novel. He will never know he already has graduated. The professor no longer teaches for us. I don't blame anyone who criticized the old programme.' Ben meant it as a compliment to the new one. 'I care about the quality of the programme.'

Pilkington's lips were wet from the wine and he set down the glass.

'I care about it in everything I do,' Ben said.

'So do I. And I knew that about you.'

Ben picked up a fork, turned it over, then laid it back on the white cloth. He sipped the wine, too. 'From where you are, you know how the whole university runs. I – '

'That, too has stories that would surprise you. But I don't believe in running from problems. All my life I've stayed and worked things out. You'd be shocked what running a number of programmes requires. If you hadn't called me for lunch, I would have called you a little later. I've been thinking about you even though you haven't heard from me. You must have heard rumours about changes – programmes going over to different sponsorship. Of course all graduate programmes will be in the graduate school as well as the sponsor department. You must have wondered about yours.'

Ben nodded, listening.

'I hope that you will tell me about any concerns that you have.'

'Nona and I had a conversation that I'd like to tell you about. I can speak honestly to you?'

'I hope so, but not everyone does.'

'I have to,' Ben said. He glanced up, noticing the waitress. 'I guess we should order.' Ben put the red napkin in his lap and drank from the glass while Pilkington ordered. Then he did. He watched the waitress leave. 'I don't want to bring my problems to you,' he continued. 'I know that my job is to run the programme. I'll do that. But I'm worried about Nona.'

'She's a strong woman,' Pilkington said. 'And I'm putting pressure on her.'

'I admire her. I think anyone has to. But I care more about the quality of my programme than I do about the size of her budget.' He wiped his lips with the napkin and put it on his legs. 'When I told her how many Phi Beta Kappas had applied for next year, she said she wasn't sure we wanted Phi Beta Kappas. She said she wants people coming back to school part-time. Non-conventional students. "We don't want Phi Beta Kappas," she said.'

'I'm not surprised,' Pilkington said. 'Are you? Nona has done a lot as Dean. And the President has given her a good deal of aggravation this year. She has real cause to worry.'

'But she will change the programme however she has to to keep it,' Ben said. 'You know our surplus. She'll take it all and change the programme so that it can't prosper.'

'Everyone has been very happy with what you've accomplished. Nona, too. She's in a difficult position. So are you.'

'I'd rather leave than let her change things her way.'

'Don't even think of leaving,' Pilkington said. 'That's why I wanted to talk to you.'

'I want the programme moved out of her supervision. I want out of it. I don't want to be in the middle.'

'Give me a day or two. All right?'

'I like the university,' Ben said. 'I don't want to leave.' He swallowed and set down the empty glass. He hadn't meant to say that.

'You know something just crossed my mind that might interest you. We've just received a small amount of money – not enough – but it is targeted to help subsidize faculty housing. It's to help us keep good people that the university needs. I can't promise, but I could recommend you for a special loan. I believe the highest amount is for one hundred thousand, and it's six per cent interest for ten years.'

'I would be interested,' Ben said.

'I'm glad I thought of you then. I can't say definitely, but you certainly should qualify as head of the programme.'

'Thank you,' Ben said. Please do it, he thought. And please get Nona off my tail. You're the only one who can.

Ben walked back toward his office, full, the wine comfortable in his stomach and head. Pilkington made a difference. It was like a miracle for Pilkington to agree. It made all kinds of things possible for the moment. And he was grateful.

The tinted-glass windows of the three-storey building ahead shone darkly. Ben walked up the steps to the entrance and opened the door. He went to the pay phone in the carpeted foyer. He dropped in a quarter, listened for the bell, and dialled.

'Sylvia?'

'Where are you?' Her voice blared.

'I'll be there in half an hour.'

'Are you still at lunch?'

'Have there been any calls?'

'Have there? And Daryl wants to meet with you as soon as you get back.' She lowered her voice. 'I told him you might not get back. And I have something to tell you that's private.'

'In half an hour,' he said. 'Thanks.' Then he put the phone on the hook and looked across the foyer of the building where he stood. It was the entrance to the large gymnasium.

On top of the purple carpet, silver and gold trophies of State were displayed. Only this glare and the lettering on the President's office made him feel like a visitor on campus. He relaxed, feeling the wine. Three students passed and he watched them.

He sat deeply on one of the blue benches and glanced at the folders he had carried. He noticed at once that Sylvia had misspelled Pilkington's name on one. Ben began to peel off the label.

He yawned. No one could call him here. No one was outside the door waiting. He looked at the shining gold and silver. He relaxed, feeling good.

The closest trophy was nearly as tall as he was and looked valuable. Beside it, a gilt one had just been polished. Is anyone here, he thought, who has won one of these? Across the room a student slept on a long bench. He looked tired. Had the trophies put him to sleep? Got him dreaming? Two more students were entering the glass front doors and had come to praise the displays. He could see the immediate impression the trophies made on them.

If I had won any, he thought, which one would I want? He looked at them more closely. Engraved silver, braised gold, polished bronze. He liked an ornate Bacchus cup with gold wash in the nearest display case. It was for – track, first place, 20 metre race. 1968. He had been thirty years old then. Below it was a plaque that he read – he leaned closer – third place in varsity swimming. It was tarnished around the engraving. Not that one. The next one was a massive football trophy with a gold player on top. Then a tall, simple silver cup. Track.

Ben sat back, interested. He thought that he should hurry. Daryl was waiting. He looked again at the trophies and he wished he had one. Something he had accomplished in his own hands. My life is dramatically different from the lives of the people who put this room together, he thought. Where are they? How long had the races lasted for them? Listen, he thought, I would have liked it, too. He thought of all the courses he had taken, the books from the library shelves that boasted a million. He could have read until he died, he thought, and never have won a single trophy.

'Did you go to lunch by way of New York City?' Sylvia asked. She cocked her eyes, the balls not pretty. The cups of her breasts were pooched, as if her nipples, under the purple stretched halter, might explode at him. He was glad that she wore the gold tank-size belt, the purple pants that draped her hips.

'Sylvia, much of my business is at lunch,' he said.

'Mine too,' she said. 'And I'm on a diet.' She raised her brows and lowered her soft voice. 'What I wanted to tell you was that Barbara told Daryl that our office disturbs the whole floor.'

'She what?'

'She said that the phone isn't answered at lunch. And that no one is here at eight. Daryl asked me what time Chuck gets here in the morning.'

'What did you say?'

'I had to tell him. Ten o'clock.'

'Did you say that he stays until eight at night because Nona wants the evening covered?'

'He didn't ask,' she said.

'Did you talk to Barbara?'

'That bitch?'

'I don't believe the phones should be answered during lunch,' he said. 'The programme has to rest. Businesses shouldn't always be open.' He waited for her to agree but she didn't. 'We're people,' he said, 'and businesses should act human. Let them rest.' She glanced away. 'Otherwise,' he continued, 'we're a machine.' Oh God, why did he try to explain? It was personal. Wasn't he boss? 'I'll see Barbara and tell her that my office is none of her business. If hers were busy, she wouldn't be so nosy.'

'Her secretaries never have anything to do,' Sylvia said.

'See?'

'Well, why do I have to work when they don't?' She sat with a smack against the wide office chair. 'I'd rather read books, too.'

'Tell Daryl that about Barbara, then.'

'And have him mad at me?' She opened the desk drawer and took out a Mars bar which he watched her unwrap and bite into.

'Would you get the file of new applicants, please, and this year's budget? I'm going to tell Daryl something I've been saving.'

'Where did you put it?' she asked.

Ben said nothing. He walked to the file cabinet and opened it.

'Oh, I'll find it,' she said. 'Honestly, men are such babies.'

Ben hurried to his office, shut the door, leaned far back in the chair and put his feet on the desk.

A minute later, the door banged open and Sylvia's breasts took several minutes to stop heaving. Her purple nails at her nipples, she took a deep breath. 'I found them all,' she said.

'Thank you.'

'Any time. I'm the only one who knows where anything is around here. Can I get off at four, please? It's important.'

Ben nodded. Then as she was leaving, he asked, 'Is the office covered?'

'Why do you think I asked you?'

'Then you can't,' he said.

She glared, huffed out and slammed the door.

Ben looked at his watch. Daryl was waiting. He opened the file and began to take notes. Exactly what he would point out. Then he got up, straightened his tie and left.

'One minute, please,' Daryl said as Ben stood in the doorway to the office.

'Fine.' Ben stepped back into the hall. He looked into the

small receptionist office that had been converted from a storage room. It had no window.

'How're you?' Corrine asked. She rolled her eyes, her finger pointing toward the next room. 'He isn't busy really.'

'I don't care,' Ben said. He stepped back toward Daryl's, the thick folder in his hand.

'Come in,' Daryl finally called. He held a framed photograph of his twin daughters, dressed in ruffles. 'I was worried you wouldn't get back.'

'My afternoon is already scheduled,' Ben said. 'I don't have long.'

Daryl shook his head yes, then pressed the intercom button. 'Corrine, please hold my calls,' he said.

'I always do when you're in conference,' she said.

'Except for the Dean.'

'Of course, everyone but Amazon lady.'

'I think that she might call, all right?'

'Do you want me to bring in coffee?'

'No, thanks,' Ben put in. 'Not for me.'

Daryl said no, then hung up, and swivelled his chair around, quickly.

'Before we begin –' Ben said.

Daryl looked up, surprised.

'I have something to show you.'

Daryl's eyelids rose, his lips curling. 'Of course.'

'Oh, you'll like it.'

Daryl nodded, his tongue against the corner of his lips.

'These figures – ' Ben stopped and handed him the notes. 'I told you that our profit would be twelve to eighteen thousand higher this term. I've know that was low. I wasn't sure how much higher until now. It's at least thirty-eight thousand or more for the semester. That's over one hundred twenty thousand profit for the year after costs are subtracted.' He could feel his hand shaking. 'Of course we need about seven thousand to finish this term. There's forty-five thousand in the accounts.'

'Oh. That is good news.'

'Some of it should be fed back into the programme. For recruitment.'

'You say that you need seven thousand more this term?' Daryl wrote it down. 'Tell me – if you didn't have the, say, thirty thousand extra profit, would you be seven thousand in the red?'

'It's not in the red. That's seven thousand out of the forty-five profit.'

'But without the thirty-eight profit would you be that much in the hole?'

'I don't think that matters.' Ben took out his pen and scooted his chair by Daryl's. He noticed that Daryl had spilled ketchup on his shirt and that the cuffs had heavy wear at the hems. He pointed to the forty-five thousand. 'That's the gross amount we have.'

'The seven thousand subtracted from it leaves the profit – thirty-eight thousand.'

'But without the thirty-eight thousand would you be in the red?' Daryl repeated.

'There is no such thing as without it.' Ben sat up, abnormally close to Daryl's face. He saw several moles on his chin he hadn't noticed and a thick muscle at his neck.

'You see I'm worried about your expenses. I'm glad your profit is even more than we thought. The Dean will be glad to hear it too. It doesn't affect our situation. I believe the seven thousand means that there is some fat in your programme somewhere.'

'The new classes that you started for your programme didn't make,' Ben said. 'You lost eighteen thousand. I didn't.'

'No. We knew we might have to run them a time or two first.' Daryl shook his finger, pointing. 'There's no need to get upset again, Ben.'

'Well, I am upset.'

'I asked you about expenses, not profit.'

Ben glanced out the window at the traffic cop below. The man directed traffic all day. Why don't you come up and arrest him, he wondered. Take him away.

'Don't leave yet,' Daryl said. 'One more quick thing, then I have an appointment.'

Ben sat back down.

'Someone – and I won't say who, has made a complaint about your office. Evidently the phone disturbs the other offices early in the morning and at noon. Is someone supposed to open at eight?'

'Barbara has no business in my office,' Ben said. 'If she would shut her door she couldn't hear anything.' He stood up, his eyes widening. 'I run my office,' he said. 'As long as I make a profit – the largest in the college – you should leave me alone. You should be glad.'

'I'm very glad. Ben, you'd be surprised. I go around campus saying wonderful things about you. And not only to the Dean.'

'Because what I do makes you look good. If you ran it, the programme would lose money just as yours does.'

Daryl shook his head, grinning, licking his front upper teeth. 'You're getting upset again,' he said.

'Of course I am. You tell Barbara that I'm making an inspection of her office at eight in the morning. Sylvia says that Barbara's secretaries never do anything but read. There's nothing for them to do.'

'I'll tell Barbara that I spoke with you,' Daryl said. 'There's no need for you – '

'No. *I'll* tell her exactly what I think.' Ben stood up. He looked a moment at Daryl's desk. The neatly stacked memos, the sharpened yellow pencils, the typewriter with a draft of a memo. The paperclips were kept in the tray, scotch tape handy, the box of ballpoints. Oh God. He knew where nothing was in his own office. Literally anything could be on the floor or under a pile of papers. He couldn't help it. The neatness distracted him from what he was doing. But he knew how to run the programme. 'I'm warning you,' Ben said. 'Don't push me.'

'No one wants to. Do you realize your xerox bill was twenty-eight dollars more than Barbara's last month? We're going to have to discuss it.'

'Barbara's programme is half the size of mine.' Ben turned and walked out the door, shutting it. He stood a moment, his anger swelling. He should go back in, and tell him off.

'Boy, you told him,' Corrine said. 'No one talks to him like that.'

'I shouldn't,' Ben said.

'He's stupid.' She giggled, her throat skinny. 'I've worked for a lot of people and he's the most stupid by far. I could tell you things he's said to other people. Everybody hates him.'

'How do you stand it?' Ben asked.

'Listen, I tell him what to do. He gives me the slightest trouble and I'm out of this office. You think I need this job? I can walk out of here this minute and go to work at my old job in the morning.' She lowered her voice to a whisper. 'I have an interview next Tuesday. I've already told him if I get the job I'm quitting this one.'

'Don't quit,' Ben said.

'I sure will.'

'I will, too.' He waved 'bye and hurried down the hallway. Before he thought, he was bent over the water fountain, his mouth full of water, his lips touching the metal. Germs. He jerked up and continued to his office, shaking.

'It's Vice President Pilkington on two,' Chuck said. 'And Howard Israel called from Dallas. He'll call back. And Dale Smith called.'

Ben pressed two. 'Hello,' he said. 'I enjoyed our lunch.'

'I did too. I think I have good news about a loan. There is a bit left, and we just might get the hundred thousand.'

'That's marvellous,' Ben said.

'I'll look into it further,' Pilkington said.

'Thank you,' Ben said. He hung up. Wouldn't owning his own home make a difference? Good news had wandered in, logically suggesting improvements. Why on earth hadn't he thought of them? Or of going to Pilkington about a house?

He hurried from his office, went down the hallway past Barbara's open door, to Danz's. Ben walked in as he knocked.

'Daryl and I just talked,' Danz said, 'that bastard.' He screwed the lid back on his fountain pen and clipped it into his shirt pocket. He got up, walking over to the sofa where Ben sat.

Ben could hardly hear him when he began to whisper. 'Please don't repeat this, although I feel like everyone knows. Daryl and Nona have decided that Barbara should be Director here. They're making up some new job that won't have any authority for me.'

'Daryl told you this?'

'It will only cost them money to promote her and cut me.'

'He told you that they are thinking of this?' Ben never would have cut Danz. It was insanity. Danz was their most competent administrator.

'It's already done. The 31st of the month she is Director.' He lit a cigarette, puffed, then began to finger the gold-coloured lighter. 'I can't help wondering about some of the things she said to me.'

'She won't threaten him,' Ben said. 'He can tell her what to do. He'd love to see me go, too.'

'I'll be switched to half pay on the 1st.'

'Don't quit,' Ben said.

'I'm not.'

'He knows you were a finalist for his job.'

Danz leaned back, then loosened his striped tie. 'What am I supposed to do?' He put his feet up on the coffee table. 'He's asked me to help him prepare next year's budget because Barbara doesn't have experience.'

Ben left and glanced at his watch. Then he went back to his office, locked it and went to his car.

As he crossed the overpass that led to the freeway access, he looked out at the divided eight lane. Cars buckled down the freeway and wouldn't let it move. Happy birthday, he told himself. Their exhaust almost hid them and billowed. The bumpers, fenders, car tops, grilles, doors, and windshields could only have gotten so squeezed by every driver inching forward.

Ben turned on to the access road and got in line. He made Patsy Cline louder on the radio and watched the driver of the car ahead looking for a moment to enter the traffic.

The engine of the car behind him revved. Once, twice, louder. Suddenly it roared, the wheels moving, then brakes squealed. Ben glanced in the rear view mirror. The bright car had stopped just before hitting him. Ben shrugged. He looked at the dust on the dashboard.

The rent would be raised six per cent in two months. About forty-five dollars. They couldn't afford what it already was. He inched up, with the car ahead. He had another year on the instalments to the dentist and the American Express was two months past due. He would give Alice his receipt so that she could check the payroll deductions. Something had to be wrong with them.

In Santa Monica, he drove down Fifth toward Montana. The apartments and condos that he passed were alike. There was too much stucco and brick on the lighted palm-lined streets, the thin strip of grass island green in front. The driveways between them brightened with sunlight and he could smell the ocean three blocks away. Ocean Hideaway. Tall Palms. The Imperial. Moon Raker. The Victoria. The Pacific. The Majestic Arms.

Ben drove along Third and passed a small white house that was now waiting between two condos. Lilies and yellow daffodils grew in the flowerbed in front. The condo next door had a half-circle entrance into a dim foyer. The green stucco had gotten sick, and affected all the weathered furniture and towels on the black wrought iron balconies. The white, corner condo building had tall windows, underground parking, and a glass entrance planted with flowers.

Every apartment was occupied. He and Alice had looked when they first came, but none allowed children. He had sneaked looks into the managers' apartments, however, and they were all alike, filled with cooking and furniture moved from other places where they had lived.

These apartments were more like large motel rooms with people coming and going. Their automobiles filled the parking spaces, the garages. The red brick condo at the end of Third was bigger and newer than any. A tan Rolls was parked at the entrance, under the eye of a uniformed chauffeur. Oversized chandeliers inside the lobby shone against the tall mirrored walls. Ben looked up at the layers of apartments with narrow curved balconies.

He turned right on Montana. The liquor store had customers, the Rexall with good breakfasts had shut down, and the shops selling antiques, clothes, quiches, and toys were closing. He stopped at a red light, the library where he took Jules for story-telling across the street. In a minute he was at 26th and turned right.

Happy birthday, he told himself, a block from his house. He saw her parents' grey Chevy. They had already arrived. The grey car was like a warning. Ben pulled in behind it and stopped. OK. My hands are in the air, he thought. Don't shoot.

He could see them through the little glass pane in the door. Hershel was sunken into the green sofa, his glasses shiny, his cheeks fat, his red hair, threads. He glanced up toward Ben. When their eyes caught, Ben felt a tug at his lip.

Hershel's smile made him look like a fisherman who had just got lucky.

Olita sat across from Alice on one of the pumpkin-coloured silk chairs. They appeared to be talking as if practising a language, their smiles as uneasy as their voices. Olita's appearance was so circumspect as to be instantly noticeable. Everything about her was neat and little. Her light hair slightly curled, her lips almost pink, her eyes hazel under the thin lashes. Her expression as she looked up was pleasant and contrasted with her face.

'Well, surprise,' Olita said, slowly.

'Hello.' Alice crossed the room to kiss him. Her nervousness made her completely different. He noticed perspiration on her cheeks.

Ben grinned at Jules who sat on the sofa and held out his arms. 'Daddy! Daddy! Daddy!'

'Hey!' Ben leaned over, kissing him. He hugged Jules gently.

'How was Vice President Pilkington?' Alice asked.

'Fine.'

'We saw your yard,' Olita said. 'The flowerbeds sure are pretty.'

'Aren't they?' Ben said.

'They sure are,' Hershel said as if they weren't and nodded. 'They sure are. Got a lot of people in California, don't you?'

Ben didn't answer.

'About how many are there?' Hershel cleared his throat and began to grin.

'I don't know. The whole state is overpopulated because it's so nice,' Ben said.

'Uh huh. Nice, huh?' He laughed loudly. 'I never understood why everyone liked California so much.'

'It's beautiful, Daddy,' Alice said.

He nodded.

'You remember our vacation to San Francisco?'

Hershel nodded again.

'You've got a real pretty house,' Olita said.

Ben looked from the flowers on the mantel to the open beige curtains and outside the blinds at the traffic on 26th. With so many cars, weren't people he didn't want to see bound to pull into his drive? Weren't these better than some? He lifted Jules, putting him on his legs.

'Are you hungry?' Alice asked.

He nodded. If they'd liked me, he thought, you wouldn't have married me. What do you expect?

Olita got up too, taking the glasses and the fancy napkins from the table. He watched her smooth her white skirt, then walk from the room.

He didn't like being a snob, but they didn't like him.

What was left of the room was not big enough for Hershel and him. The walls narrowed and shortened. The furniture shrank. Ben leaned back against the thick cushion and closed his eyes. Then he got up, sat on the orange carpet and began to stack Jules's blocks. 'Want to make a fort?' he asked. 'Come on.'

'Yes.' Jules sat beside him, leaned over, taking hold of two blocks. One fell from his small fist.

'Yes sir, California sure is overcrowded,' Hershel said. 'I've never seen so many people.'

The blocks had letters on one side and numbers on the other. They were smaller and made of cheaper wood than Ben remembered his to be. Ben held one against his nose, sniffing.

'How do you get paid, Ben?' Hershel asked.

Ben hesitated then decided to try it. 'Every month.'

'Oh?' Hershel nodded, crossing his feet, his black shoes shaped like irons. 'Couldn't they pay you every week?'

Ben took a blue block roughly in his hands without looking up. 'Why?'

'Every thirty days?' Hershel whistled.'That's a long time. No wonder you have trouble budgeting.'

155

Ben began to list what they owed them: over $3,000 plus some interest, borrowed over three years.

'About how much do you clear?' Hershel asked.

Ben saw the thin lips parted enough for light to leak through Hershel's teeth. Here was clearly something obscene that was not sexual.

'You don't have to tell me,' Hershel said.

'I'm not going to.' Ben stacked the blocks in rows of five, with one between every two at the next layer and the third. He could tell that Jules was listening. 'I might,' Ben said, 'but neither writers nor teachers make much. Obviously I chose both. It wouldn't be worth telling.' He could not imagine why he was grinning.

'Um hmm,' Hershel said. He ran his hand nervously across his chin. 'Ahh, how much do you really make?'

'I do well in my field,' Ben said.

'How much do you clear then?'

'How much do you?' Ben asked.

Hershel's laughter was genuine. Happy. He turned so that his shoulders faced Ben too, reached across and picked up the cup of coffee he had set on the table. He drank noisily. 'I'm not going to tell you,' he said. 'How much does it cost you to live every day?'

Ben began another row of blocks, letting half a minute pass. 'How much money does it cost?' he asked. He heard the door from the dining room to the kitchen open, then close. Alice knew he was not enjoying this. Wasn't her duty to keep them away from him since they belonged to her? He began to wonder if she was like them.

'It costs you about the same as me. Seventy-five dollars a day. I'm smart about these things. How much is your rent?'

'I don't know,' Ben said. 'Alice pays the bills.'

'Oh.' Hershel's teeth lighted again as he chuckled. 'Oh. I think you know. Have you ever thought of finding another kind of job?' Hershel reached into his shirt pocket and took out a cigarette, flicked his lighter and puffed. 'I'd look around for something else to do if I were you.'

Ben looked up and took a revolver out of his brain. He aimed it dead centre. Bang. Hershel said nothing.

'I think they're hiring at the defence plant in Grand Prairie,' Hershel said.

'You should apply,' Ben said.

'I'd sure think about it if I were you.'

'I don't think college administration is such a terrible career. Most people don't think so. Or writing. They have some prestige.'

'Oh?' Hershel chuckled, puffing. 'I wouldn't know about prestige,' he said.

'I don't think I'm doing so bad,' Ben said. Saying it made him realize that he was. 'I'm doing better than you were at my age,' he said angrily.

'I don't know,' Hershel said. He spoke louder and slowly. 'I sure don't.' He reached back and scratched behind one of his big white ears.

'I do.'

'I never asked anyone for a dime,' Hershel said. 'I'd sure have found me a better way to make a living before I did. I'd never have asked my father-in-law for money. I'd have gotten me a responsible job.'

Ben let the row of blocks he was building fall.

'Daddy, let's build it again,' Jules said.

'OK.' He began to stack them. He could smell Italian sauce: onions, cucumbers, tomatoes. He could see them dripping down Hershel's cheeks, tomatoes reddening the already orange hair.

Ben placed a yellow block on top.

'Daddy!' Alice said.

Ben looked up. Neither of them had heard her come into the room.

'I've just been asking him a few questions.'

'You're being insulting. I heard you.'

Hershel grinned, rubbing his palm over his lips.

The snob in Ben began to rise above them, as if he had died. Go, it said, please. Open your eyes and leave this place, Ben. If you say anything, you're rude. Get up, leave. Then he is being rude.

Ben reached over and kissed Jules quickly. 'I love you,' he said.

'I love you,' Jules said.

Ben got up, brushed lint from his slacks and walked into the hallway. He opened and shut the bathroom door, but did not go in. On the comfort in their room was a wrapped package with a brown bow. The Happy Birthday paper was striped brown and black. Next to it was a book, in a plastic bag. Ben picked it up as he left.

In Jules's room, toys were on the pillows, in the rocker, on the carpet. Ben stepped over them and unlocked the sliding glass door. He made as little noise as he could. Outside, the patio awning blocked the moon, but he could see the flowers, the playhouse, Jules's wagon and tricycle.

Olita stood at the kitchen sink and ran water.

Ben hurried to the walk and looked back at the house. His pulse was as angry as he was.

It was wrong for Hershel to accuse him of exactly what his worst fears were. Did he do that to Hershel, ever? No. Because no one knew about anyone else. Everything inside him was fresh and the first time. Everything he thought rang a bell in his head, every curious moment was packed into his brain, every love he felt in his heart. No one could ever jump ahead of what he thought. It was his purpose.

He walked down the drive quietly. The lights on, Hershel was deeper in the sofa, up to his ears. He was smiling, trying to cool Alice down.

Ben started the Honda, put it in reverse, pressed on the gas, and backed out.

Freedom was on the bottom of his foot.

He couldn't think of anywhere better than *out*. He left *in* to Hershel. The lights on the boutiques, the restaurants, storey after storey of highrises, and the bright cars marked a runway. He was in flight. Had they discovered him yet? Would they slowly rearm and turn on each other?

Glancing back, Ben would not have been surprised to see a flaming explosion. He continued to Ocean, followed the Mercedes convertible in front, and glimpsed the dark and shiny ocean beyond Palisades Park. Baskin Robbins was bright, a police helicopter whirred over, shining down its floodlights.

He drove past the Santa Monica pier, then rows of apartment houses. The Venice marker was a mile away. He passed it. When he saw the Paris Theatre marquee, the parking lot filling, he decided what to do. The marquee read 'Third World Beauty Contest.' Ben pulled in, parked, and bought a ticket.

He sat inside the lighted auditorium and sipped the glass of wine he had bought in the lobby. The intimate audience was laughing even before the film started. Ben looked back, seeing an obese woman enter, swinging a pink boa, her hair like duck feathers. The people in front of her giggled. One man whistled and the woman began to flaunt her enormous bust. As she passed Ben he noticed that she was a man, the fat falling over the waistband. The next customer wore aluminium foil for a bathing suit with a matching foil hat. Then a man entered wearing tiger skin shorts and carrying a club. He began to grunt, finding a seat. Another man, made up to imitate Marilyn Monroe with a big smile, walked quickly in, then a woman dressed in a suit and made up with a moustache like Groucho.

Ben settled back. He would have preferred a classic movie that he knew he would like, regardless of the audience. He stretched, nervous from arguing with Hershel. The lights darkened; the wine velvet curtains spread. The movie set was a beauty contest stage.

On screen Miss Piss entered and squatted, got up, screamed, squatted, then wiggled. He had heavy yellow eyeshadow and wet long hair with yellow liquid dripping down his back. 'Miss Piss,' the moderator announced as the audience on film applauded first.

Ben kept expecting him to piss, but no. Instead a huge transvestite came on stage, his curls falling, his great dress frayed. Ben liked him. The deep voice, the enormous hips, kicking up. Then a metal person was announced, antennae sticking from an aluminium hat, gloves, shoes, and aluminium plate for a dress. He walked slowly across the stage, the coloured cinema lights reflecting on the costume.

By the next contestant Ben understood that the purpose was never to be authentic anyway. Each was trying to be overdone, not a joke but an exaggerated imitation of what someone like that would be in bad taste.

He disliked any idea suggesting that people with bad taste weren't serious. Wasn't it very bad taste to try to enjoy bad taste?

He had better call Alice. He got up from the velour seat and hurried to the lobby. The pay telephone was on the wall beside the women's room. He put a quarter into the slot.

'Hello?' Alice answered on the first ring.

'I'm at a movie,' he said.

'I didn't know you had gone until a minute ago. I told Daddy he was rude.'

He was relieved Alice wasn't angry with him.

'Jules is crying because you left. Will you talk to him?'

'I didn't think I should stay and argue.'

'They're leaving,' Alice said. 'I told Daddy – '

'That would make me wrong. Tell them I'm staying in a motel. I'll meet you and Jules for breakfast.'

'How was your lunch with Pilkington?'

'OK. I'll tell you in the morning.'

'What movie are you at?'

'In Venice,' he said. 'I'm sorry, but – '

'It's not your fault. Daddy was awful. Jules told him he was, too. Mother said that Daddy never insulted anyone and I told her that he certainly did. Then Daddy said that he was sorry if you took it wrong. They're in the kitchen washing dishes. They were planning to leave in the morning.'

'That's fine,' Ben said. 'I'll call you later, OK?'

'OK,' Alice said.

Ben hung up, and went back into the pitch dark auditorium. A man thirty feet high on the screen had bobbie pins in his hair and was dressed like a housewife. He carried a small vacuum, took a second, bent over and touched the hose against his rear end. He gave a quick start. Then he giggled and held up the hose for applause.

Ben wished that Hershel and Olita could watch. Their shock would be a successful example of what the contest was about.

The audience would love Olita and Hershel. The two could steal the show without changing an iota. Olita could begin to clear the stage and Hershel could either sit and watch TV or talk about anything out loud. Ben shook his head, the truth too much. He looked at his watch, then went to the lobby for more wine.

At ten he saw the Aku Aku motel off Ocean, parked by the lighted office and went in. The carpet was waterstained where it met the glass window and needed sweeping. A brass cuspidor at the end of the registration counter was used for a waste basket. The clerk slept at a desk, his face resting on his arms. Ben stood at the counter and glanced at the photographs displayed. There were five. Each showed a celebrity that Ben thought he should recognize. Had these people stayed at the motel? He doubted it. Someone like Diana Dors in a tight dress, a man beaming, his arm around her, was in one; a dark-haired starlet laughed in the next and everyone sat around a nightclub table. Beside these, a print of the Santa Monica pier had been left crooked and contrasted with the painted wall. The large picture window was streaked and the yellow drapes sagged.

'Do you have a vacancy?' Ben asked. The motel had probably been new in the Fifties and sort of fancy. The desk clerk opened his eyes and sat up. He nodded.

Ben paid for the night and walked outside and along the drive. He carried the key in one hand and the plastic bag with the book in the other. Number 81 faced the garbage bin in the alley. Its doorknob wiggled as Ben turned the key, then pushed. He flipped on the light.

The half bed had no spread and was crowded in the room. Ben shut the door as he stepped in. He put the book he had brought on the bed table. The TV blocked the mirror on the dresser. He lay down on the bed, feeling a plastic mattress cover under the sheet.

He looked at the thin orange curtains over the window, the scratches on the back of the door, the glass ashtray with a beer advertisement set on top of the bed table. The pillow had a plastic cover, too.

Someone turned over in bed in the next room.

He had just paid forty-two dollars for a bed that he wouldn't have slept in at home.

The man and woman next door began to talk. Ben tried not to listen. She was loudly describing a screenplay that she wanted to write.

Sometimes it depressed him to think of things that people wanted to do. It reminded him of things that he had wanted to do. Of reasons that he did things. He should tell Howard that.

He tried to get comfortable.

What if he got to choose all over again what career he would have. Would he ask Hershel's opinion?

He would do *what he wanted*.

He wanted to write books, publish and have an audience. Was that silly? He opened his eyes, the voices in the next room clear. It was so hard and he hadn't understood and wouldn't have listened to anyone's advice. You don't need an audience, he thought. You just need to write and listen. It was the most personal of choices. It involved personal successes.

He turned over, then took out the book.

THE MALE MID-LIFE CRISIS. It was from Alice. He opened it, finding the list of contents. *Case studies. Ambition and the middle-aged male. Impotence. The Younger Woman syndrome. Do you have a mid-life crisis?* Do I have a mid-life crisis? he asked. *Page 184..* He thumbed through the pages, glimpsing sentences. *Howard Smith, 44, was passed over for a promotion at Del Monte after 18 years as a district manager . . . The first time that I cheated on Elaine occurred just after an argument on our vacation to Hawaii . . . page 122 . . . Communication between husband and wife is essential if the marriage is to hold together . . . Page 184. Do you have a Mid-Life Crisis?* He ran his finger down the symptoms. *Are you unhappy with your job?* Yes. *Do you feel confused about your life because your goals don't seem as possible?* Yes. *Have you paid less attention to your wife in the past year?* Yes. *Do you feel that your responsibilities are now all long-term ones?* Yes. *Do they tie you down?* Yes. Yes. *Do you find yourself more critical of others than usual?* Yes.

He was forty. He was facing an ending that did not make him feel close to anyone. *If depression occurs, the middle-aged man should see a doctor immediately. Statistics show that the male suicide rate increases dramatically during the years 40–50.*

Ben looked up at the ceiling, the plastic light globe dim. He closed his eyes. The bed squeaked as he turned over, his face on his arms. He put the pillow across his eyes. He wouldn't dream of condemning people for their work or what they wanted.

I probably am having a mid-life crisis, he thought. He turned to the case studies, more interested.

George Stephens had spent his working career as a journalist at the *Milwaukee Sun*. He had expected to become editor-in-chief and possibly publisher because for years he had won more major awards than anyone on the paper.

When Edwin Schevill retired, George was prepared to accept the offer from the publisher, Bob Wilson. But Wilson felt that George did not get along well enough with others to manage the paper, no matter how well he wrote. George was passed over for the first time in his life. He left work a minute after he heard, went to the Circus Bar down the street from the paper, and didn't go home that night. Ellen Stephens found out what had happened by calling a friend at the paper and asking where George was.

George came home the next afternoon, in a new Corvette. He had shaved his beard and bought a two hundred dollar pair of sunglasses. He had a ticket to Acapulco and told Ellen that he was not sure when he would return.

Six months later he still had not looked for another job, their joint savings were getting low and Ellen was making all decisions for the family, which included two boys in high school. George spent all day drinking beer in his study and working on a novel. He told her that he had always wanted to write a novel, that he should never have worked for a newspaper and that he was changing his life for the good. He would not miss this chance.

Ellen left him eight months later and moved herself and the boys into an apartment. They had sold their house and at the time of the interview she had not seen George for several weeks.

Ben took a deep breath. Poor George.

He turned the page. Carl Brown from Arlington, Texas, sold his printing company although it was doing well. His business manager, who did most of the work anyway, was eager to buy, at a price that satisfied them both. Carl said he was bored, did not feel he needed the income because of real estate he had bought, and wanted more time to himself. He had turned forty-three. Six months after the sale, he started a publishing company and sold two of his four rent houses to finance the package. He published twelve books in eight months and needed more capital. Against the advice of his wife Jan, Carl sold the other two rent houses and put the money into his new venture. The company showed a small profit, but Carl and Jan could not keep up the lifestyle that they had grown used to. Jan got her real estate licence, and with a housing boom in Arlington, made two sales her first month. Carl meanwhile agreed to publish four more books – this time religious ones. He made a radical religious conversion and decided to sell the publishing company and attend a Baptist seminary in Fort Worth. Jan was trying to support the family by her career in real estate.

Ben laid down the book. Oh my God, he thought. Poor Carl. It made him feel sorry for himself.

Maybe I should go make money, he thought. Was he really tied to Daryl and Nona and to State? Was he just going through middle age? Happy birthday, he thought.

7

Breakfast

The next morning Ben sat in a tangerine restaurant booth, gigantic photographs of bacon and eggs framed on the walls. He watched a plate of buttered hot cakes carried past, then sipped from his glass of water, sucking in a small piece of ice. Outside the window, cars on Pico flashed in the sunlight. Alice and Jules would show up any minute.

He liked being up and out, his job across town. The coffee steamed; the line at the register grew. A man in the booth behind him began laughing noticeably. The dining room was a hodgepodge of busyness, like he was when he was in a hurry.

He wasn't, though. And he felt clear-headed. 'I think it's good to talk to stupid people,' William had told him once. 'You have to be simple, and it can make you understand what you think more clearly.'

What Ben disdained most about Hershel was his refusal to like anything Ben did. It wasn't that Hershel disliked him. Hershel *blamed* him. Ben knew about feelings that grew very privately in families. These emotions held special attitudes without having to be reasonable. They caused people to refuse to listen to each other. Hershel *enjoyed* disapproving of him.

He sipped the steaming coffee. He looked about the restaurant, ignoring the customers. Hershel was wrong, anyway. People didn't fail in *life*. They failed in what they wanted. Life was an open eye view of the moment, including neither the past or the future. In one second something could happen to change everything. Any moment made new things inevitable. Nothing escaped. Ben sat back, the sun in his eyes, light falling across the table. He glanced at a woman who looked quickly away.

Ben noticed a tan Porsche in the used car lot at the corner where Alice would pass. They would be walking along the houses that he knew too, small painted stucco ones, with grassy yards and flowers underneath the windows. Every other block was all apartment buildings. Come on, he thought, I love you.

8

Howard's Call

'Oh, Ben,' Daryl said, looking up from his work, surprised. He motioned toward the papers on his desk. 'I don't have time to meet with you.'

'You look busy.' Ben put his hand against the door-frame and took a breath of air.

Daryl's pleasure was obvious. He seemed to be trying to hide the big smile on his face.

'How are your daughters?' Ben asked.

'Sit down a minute,' Daryl said. He scooted back his office chair and faced Ben. His Phi Beta Kappa key swung from the centre of his tie chain. 'I got in late,' he said, 'because I had to talk to Grace's teacher.'

'Before school?' Ben asked.

'Yes. And I have to pick her up. She's spending the night with me.'

Ben crossed his legs, the chair seat uncomfortable. He saw Grace's picture in the small frame on the desk. 'This morning I promised to take Jules and a friend to Disneyland to celebrate my birthday.'

'We went two weeks ago,' Daryl said. He rubbed his palm over his lips, then he smiled, too. 'I know that you've been taking some of the things I've said to you personally,' Daryl said. 'I don't always speak for myself. A lot of people don't want to hear what I say.'

Ben decided not to say anything.

'I think you and I can get along, Ben,' Daryl said. 'We can communicate with each other.'

'I think we argue a lot. And you're in a good mood.'

'Yes, I am.'

'I'm glad.'

Daryl chewed his bottom lip a second, then chuckled. He took a deep breath. 'I can tell you this, Ben. You've probably heard rumours about Nōna's retirement. She – ' Daryl raised his eyebrows. 'I think that she *might* retire early. The big question for us is who would be her successor.'

'I'd think that you would have a good chance.'

Daryl stopped, his breathing audible. 'Why would you say that?'

He waited.

'Why do you?' Daryl repeated.

'I'd think you'd have an excellent chance if Nona has anything to say, and she does.'

It was like a flash of light between them.

'But Vice President Pilkington–' Daryl said.

'I'd think he would go along with Nona.'

'You do?'

'And if they want her out – ' Ben hesitated. 'If she's become competitive with other top administrators, then she has more power in picking a successor if she wants to.'

'You think Nona should insist on that?'

'If you want the job, I bet you can get it.'

Daryl nodded, his lips wet, his eyes watching Ben closely.

'It depends on Nona,' Ben said. 'But what does she have to lose if she's retiring anyway?' He didn't expect an answer. Daryl already had his hands on the deanship. Ben began to feel sick at his stomach.

'I won't be free all day,' Daryl said. 'Would you check with Corrine and make another appointment?'

'Of course I will.' Ben's voice sounded pleasant too. He got up, shut the door behind him as he left and walked past Corrine's office, along the hallway to his own.

'It's Howard Israel on the phone,' Chuck said. 'On three.

And don't forget your lunch. Goldman called to confirm it an hour ago.'

Ben hurried into his office and shut the door.

'Howard,' Ben said, 'how are you?' He sat in the high back chair and leaned back.

'I couldn't be better. Have you seen the market today?'

'It's up, then?'

'It's soaring. And I didn't expect you to have seen it. What I'm calling about is something that's come up here.'

Ben noticed that Howard's voice changed. It was businesslike.

'Something's happened that might interest you,' he said. 'You've heard me speak of Bill White.'

'I've met him,' Ben said. 'At Austin with you.'

'I remember that. You know he and I work closely together. On a daily basis. White's decided to go his own way, Ben. It's been going on for a while and I won't go into why. But he announced he's leaving. I'm going to need someone to take his place.'

'Oh,' Ben said.

'I don't know if you'd be interested.'

'I really wasn't asking you for a job when I called, Howard.'

'I know that. I didn't think you were. I wouldn't want to persuade you to do anything. But I hoped you'd like to come to Dallas and see us.'

'Actually things have improved here,' Ben said.

'I knew they would.'

Ben pressed down his thumb, flattening it against the desk top. 'My biggest complaint about teaching is with the money.'

'I wouldn't be surprised if the top teaching salary there is less than an MBA and a year of experience is with us.'

'I wouldn't either,' Ben said. 'Is it White's job?'

'We can talk about that. If you're interested at all, you should come right away. Several people in the company have contacted me already.'

'I need to call Alice,' Ben said. He tried to think how to ask the next quetstion. 'Howard,' he said. He knew there wasn't any easy way. 'Could you tell me what it would pay?'

'That would be up to me. In the sixties to begin.'

'I could come,' Ben said.

'When is the soonest you could?'

'Sunday. And could I come back here Monday?'

'Go ahead and make the reservations. I'll plan to pick you up at the airport, OK?'

'Fine,' Ben said. 'I'll call you back. I'll come Sunday. Tell Carolyn hello.'

Ben hung up the telephone. He hadn't meant to ask Howard for a job. They were friends.

He looked at the calendar on the wall, got a pen and marked Sunday. If he could make enough money, he might change jobs. The whole world of teaching was misunderstood because it was poor. Howard didn't understand it. Not a teacher he knew would ever make a salary as high as the bottom of the physicians, dentists, lawyers, brokers, retailers, or engineers. Much less someone with their own investment company. Didn't their low salaries make teachers look as if they didn't know better?

Teaching wasn't ever about money. He could walk into any classroom, shut the door, and come face to face with honesty. His and the students'. Writing was a way to think about that honesty. It led to how others thought and that was exciting – looking eye to eye at students and admitting that life was worth writing about. It opened up what everyone thought about their own lives.

How could a teacher tell someone off the street, driving a big car and wearing expensive clothes, that money didn't matter?

Especially when it did.

He picked up the phone and called Alice. He listened as she told him about Jules. Then he told her.

'Wouldn't it be nice to have a lot of money?' Ben asked.

'I think so.' Her voice sounded relaxed. 'We'd be good at spending it. It wouldn't be much fun if you didn't want to work in business.'

'It won't hurt to see.' he said. 'Would you make me a reservation and call me back?' He picked up his pen. 'Remember to ask Shannon to keep Jules tomorrow afternoon so we can look at houses. OK? Everyone is working in the morning.'

'I already have.'

When he hung up, he was smiling. Weren't things changing for the better? He was right to challenge Nona and Daryl. He had a possible loan to help buy a house. He bet his programme would be moved. And now, he was going to Dallas. What if he had sat back and done nothing?

He looked up as the intercom buzzed. He had to meet Goldman.

9

A Faculty Lunch

Ben arrived early at the faculty club and chose a table by the plate glass window where he could watch for David. Everyone looked hot in their fashionable suits as they crossed the garden entrance. He waved at George Howell then at Danz walking beside him. The waiter brought ice water in goblets and set down the two red menus with the gold university seal.

'He'll be here in a minute,' Ben explained and waited to order. He recognized someone at all the nearby tables – the powerful financial vice president just behind, his grey hair combed smooth; the drama chairman without a tie and eating thoughtfully; the cinema chairman at a tableful of celebrities from Hollywood. The well-known guests throughout the room were catered to by the furnishings, the red carpet, the hot silver serving dishes carried by student waiters in stiff white uniforms. It was the university's good sense to have a place to meet.

He watched as David opened the door to the garden and continued along the brick patio. Ben motioned, but David didn't notice. David had an immediate air of importance, a frown on his lips, his shoulders set back, his eyebrows raised. He was thinking deeply about something. Perspiration from the brightness was wet across his face.

Ben scooted back his chair, waiting for him to enter the dining room and join him. When David did, Ben saw the just combed hair, David's smile now genuine and sudden. He obviously was out of breath.

David sat down and patted his hand over his hair. 'That

guard at the parking lot,' he started. He picked up one of the cool glasses and sipped. 'Wouldn't let me park close by. He insisted that I go across campus. I offered to pay.'

Ben shook his head sympathetically. He had no responsibility for parking.

'I told him what I thought. *There were empty spaces directly in front of me.*'

'They're awful,' Ben said and opened the menu.

'I've never had this problem with parking where I've taught.' David picked up the menu, then laid it back. 'It's not *just* that.' He ran his fingers through his long hair, staring directly at Ben, his eyebrows twitching nervously. 'Are you even listening?'

'State is so big,' Ben said. 'It's bureaucratic.' He decided to change the subject. 'I see William and Jess this afternoon,' he said. 'Jess's going to draw me.'

David nodded and drank more water from his glass quickly. He turned, glancing at the tables nearby. Everyone was occupied. 'I'm not used to – I have a certain position or I wouldn't be teaching for you, would I?' He frowned deeply. 'I had to park half a mile away.' He picked up a spoon and let it fall, touching the knife. It made a small click. Then he unfolded his napkin and put it in his lap.

'Would you like some wine?' Ben asked.

'A coke.' David looked for the waiter, too. He sighed, scooting back his chair. 'I'm sorry. I haven't been feeling well. But this place isn't like a school.'

Ben rather agreed, but not out loud or in the faculty club. Every school was a mess because it was not just classrooms. Schools were businesses too, and some were going broke. All of them had to watch their pocketbooks. They had to keep up and build classroom buildings and stadiums and theatres. Their images were crucial to fund-raising. Who was going to teach with one hand and ask for money with the other? Schools had to have businessmen, too. They had to organize and charge for parking. No one could afford valet parking for a part-time teacher. There had to be a certain democracy, too. Didn't David realize that?

'I don't know what goes on in the classrooms,' Ben said. 'Probably a lot does. But the services *are* bad. Everyone here suffers for it. The students most of all.'

David nodded, rubbing the sleeve of his grey jacket.

The lapels were somewhat wider than the fashion and Ben didn't like the broad plaid anyway. 'I'll walk back with you when you go.'

'I like to spoil myself,' David said. 'Whenever I go to the airport I call a limousine to my front door. But I can't do that when I come to school.' His hand trembled as he picked up the glass and finished off the water.

Ben motioned to the waiter again, but both his arms were full.

'Things are so disorganized here. *Why* couldn't I park there?' He hesitated. 'And the students – you have to improve their quality. You *have* to change what *you're* doing, too.' David spoke very loudly.

Oh? Ben looked at the statement fluttering in the air. He turned his head, watching it fly past, across the room and out the door. But David had his mouth open again and something more was coming out. Ben spoke quickly.

He could see the vice president turned toward them, listening. 'Your stories you left with me are beautiful, too,' Ben said. They were, and he wanted to change the subject. 'I like them better than anything I've read in a long time.'

'They're good, aren't they? And there they are, buried in that manuscript and in a dozen magazines.'

'Something will happen with them,' Ben said.

'I think so too. I have to.' David finally caught the waiter and got him to stop. 'I'll have a coke,' he said, '*please*.'

'Maybe I should order another glass,' Ben said, and did.

He noticed David look at his watch, then pull a handkerchief from his pocket and wipe his forehead.

'I'm going to Dallas this weekend to see about a job in business,' he said, his voice light.

'You might leave?'

Ben shook his head no. 'I'll see an old friend who owns the company,' he said. 'I don't know anything about business.'

'You can't write now, can you?'

The implication was that he might consider it. Ben thought maybe he should. He looked at David's eyes and could tell that they were glassy. He had to have a fever. 'I can't leave,' Ben said. 'I have too much to do. And I've meant to tell you. John Fellows will be teaching for us next term. He specifically asked to meet you when he comes.'

David nodded slowly. 'He won the Pulitzer year before last. I've read the book.'

Ben decided against asking what he thought of it.

'I should have won in seventy-two,' David said. 'There was a woman on the committee who blocked me.' He shook his head. 'She absolutely refused to let them give it to me. How else could Rogers have won? Two on the committee had not even read his book.' He let his anger show in his face and leaned closer. 'The moment I found out that he did, I sent him a telegram.'

Ben leaned closer, too, listening. He wished that David had won. 'What did it say?' he asked.

'Four words. *You didn't deserve it.*'

'That's outrageous,' Ben said.

'Maybe not.' David pulled a handkerchief from his pocket and wiped his forehead. 'I really do feel bad,' he said. 'I'm sorry.'

'There's nothing to be sorry about,' Ben said. 'Did a judge really not even read one of the books?'

'Two of the judges hadn't read the one that won.'

For a moment, neither of them spoke. Then David's face paled, the thought too much. His head shook, his eyes closed. 'I just *can't* have lunch today,' he said. 'I'm upset. You put seventeen students in my class and promised me fourteen.'

It wasn't true. David had let in three who had asked him after everyone had registered.

'The students bring me whole novels to look at. How am I supposed to – '

'No,' Ben said. 'Tell them you can only go over what they work on this term. They know you're a writer, too. You have to be firm with them.'

'I'm very conscientious. I'm a serious teacher.'

'That's why they study with you.'

David's hands shook and he pressed them against the table. 'I mean it,' he said, 'I feel terrible.' He stood up and pushed back his chair.

Ben sat back, startled. 'David,' he spoke lowly.

'I *have* to go. You stay here.'

David hurried past the crowded tables, toward the door.

Ben tried to smile at the waiter, and hesitated a moment. Then he followed quickly across the thick carpet, out the door to the sunlight that seared his face. He did not see David directly in view.

He would have to find him. He knew how David was feeling. He opened the door leaving the courtyard. No one was on the sidewalk leading to the Chemistry building. The music school, in the opposite direction, was being remodelled and workmen had set up caution signs and pennants along the walk. David wasn't there.

Ben thought of him sitting alone somewhere. David was a wonderful writer and his friend. Did it matter if he was a prima donna? He certainly was— David could talk about his work as the greatest art and feel at home. He ran down most other writers. Above his work desk was a note he kept posted to himself. 'You do this because this is what you do. You are not jealous of others who do it.' But David was, even though he didn't want to be. He loved people. But the flaws that he saw in others' writings made him throw up his hands and wonder why people could possibly write like that.

What could publishers be thinking? There were so many writers taken under editors' arms and held up as geniuses. David could see through the advertisements, the flattering jacket blurbs, the good reviews. He cared about *his* books; his career, his audience. He cared about other people too, but they had to understand what was happening to him.

David was being ignored.

The loss of the Pulitzer was like a gunshot that tore into his heart. No operation could heal it, and the attention that he needed was constant. He was a victim. Anyone who saw him could understand that he cared. He had deserved to win.

There was no question that he had distinguished himself.

Ben saw him just ahead, sitting in a wrought iron chair on the union patio.

Ben hurried to the table and sat across, both of them in the shade of a striped umbrella.

'I mean every word that I said. I can't face class tonight.' David rubbed his forehead with both hands, his eyes closed.

'That's no problem at all,' Ben said.

'I can't read their work.'

'You shouldn't.'

'I just *can't*. I have my *own*.'

'No. You don't have to teach if you'd rather not. Take off this term; you can come back whenever you want. I'll save your place.'

David swallowed, nodding gently. 'I'd like that.'

'You're a wonderful writer,' Ben said. 'You know that I believe in you.' He did and he listened to his own soothing, praising. He noticed David's softening.

He disliked himself just a little for it.

David opened his eyes. They were dry and his lips just shaped a smile. 'I'll go on home,' he said. 'You and I can get together later. I should have called and told you I don't feel well. I'll go to my office now.'

'Of course. Come on, I'll walk with you.'

'No. I'm all right. I'll sit here a minute. Where are you going? I know you're busy.'

'To see William and Jess,' Ben said. He hesitated, then said goodbye and started off. He continued toward the faculty club. He saw one person enter, half a block ahead of him. He couldn't go in. He didn't want lunch. He walked past and along the walks, to the Philosophy building. He went up the rococo stairway to the second floor and into the small library. He sat at a marbletop table. Light came through the windows in a splash and settled across him. He had to look out, at the deep green trees, the grass, the sunlight against the leaves. What he felt was not very different from what David did.

He had feelings. He wanted to be famous, especially if everyone else he knew was going to be. He wanted to write well and be respected for, it. He looked at the rows of handsome books, the fine tables and chairs, the gilt frames, the painted ceiling. He had to try to put his life in order if he could. He faced what David did – what everybody did. It required questions.

And he did not want to be a prima donna.

Back in his office before one, Ben sat, busily going through papers. He picked up the summer schedule. He had to re-member that George Giguette was coming from Chicago to talk next week. He had to pick him up on Tuesday morning at the airport.

The intercom buzzed. Ben picked up the receiver.

'Ben?' It was Vice President Pilkington.

'How are you?' Ben said warmly.

'I've made the recommendations about moving your pro-gramme. Just as we discussed. And I spoke with Chancellor Peel. He feels that he should talk with you before he makes his final decision.'

'Of course,' Ben said.

'I made an appointment for you next Wednesday morning at nine.'

'I appreciate it,' Ben said. 'Thank you very much.'

'Thank you,' Pilkington said. 'And we discussed the loan, too. It's a definite possibility. Have you been looking at houses?'

'Yes,' Ben said. 'And they're high.' His voice sounded happy. 'I want to thank you,' he said.

10

Statistics

'Has the mail come?' Ben asked, pulling out his chair and sitting down. He stood back up and adjusted the blinds so that the sunlight didn't glare on the desk top. 'Would you bring it in?'

Chuck nodded. 'In a minute,' he said.

'I'll go through it before I start the schedule,' Ben said.

'I haven't sorted it yet.' Chuck's voice was uneasy.

'Would you bring it now?'

'I don't want to lose anything.'

'I'm not going to lose it. I'm going to look at my mail, please.'

'All right. Whatever you say.' He left the office and returned with a stack of white envelopes. 'I haven't taken out the applications or the junk mail.'

'I'll do it.' Ben turned through the envelopes. There was nothing from Dallas. Occasionally the applications were interesting. The writing samples accompanying them were often hastily written, though. Three applications had arrived, from Iowa, Texas and Maine. He had a letter form Bob Loftus. There was a printed sheet from AWP.

He ran his finger under the stapled edge and opened the folded pages. The national job list. He hadn't seen one for months. Ben glanced at the narrow entries: Kentucky had a beginning position for fiction. It only paid nineteen thousand. Ohio had an opening. South Georgia. The University of Tennessee. A senior position. He remembered the campus as rather beautiful. The salary was fine.

He wondered if he'd rather be there, out of the smog. There couldn't be traffic there. Or someone like Daryl. He bet the students were good.

The next entry was in north Alaska, making him shiver. The pay was excellent. Ben turned the page and folded it back. He looked up when Chuck walked in.

'It's the Dean's office,' he said. 'Fay needs information immediately for the Dean's meeting with Vice President Pilkington at eleven.'

'I'll take it,' Ben said. He motioned for Chuck to wait.

'Fay,' he said, picking up his phone.

Her voice was always correct. 'The Dean asked me to call. She needs some figures about your programme for her meeting at eleven. She'll be going to it from a meeting she is in now.'

'Sure,' Ben said. It was 9.40.

'She wants anything that shows an emphasis on continuing education. Are the students older? How many take only one or two classes?'

Ben wrote it down. 'All right.'

'I don't know how much you can do. She just told me what she needs. She and Daryl are in her office now. She wants you to estimate as closely as possible the number of part-time students that you have. She said be sure to include all students not admitted to the programme and only taking one or two classes, too. OK?'

'I've got it.'

'She says that she believes that many of your students are coming back to school after several years.'

'Most of them have come directly from undergraduate school,' he said. 'More of them probably should wait.'

'They'd have more experience if they did,' Fay said. 'Oh, there's my other line. Will you call me back?'

'Nona is meeting with Pilkington?'

'She has a long list to meet about. Since she asked that no one but her meet with him or President Peel she has a number of things to go over for people.'

'I didn't know she asked that.'

'Daryl will tell you if he hasn't. She wants no one to see either of them.'

'Did the Dean want to talk to me?'

'She didn't say she did,' Fay said.

He went into the outer office with Chuck and sat at the typewriter.

'She's trying to make them look like Continuing Education,' Chuck said, smirking.

'They are older.'

'They aren't any older than other grad students.'

'Check twenty. Call them out and we'll average them.'

'I'll do it. Which twenty?'

'The first twenty. Do you know how many part-time students not in the programme there are?'

'I know of two,' Chuck said. 'You shouldn't let her fake it.'

'We'll be honest.' Ben wrote down the category and two.

'How do we find out how many years they've waited to come to school?' Chuck asked.

Ben leaned over and pulled out a drawer of student files. He took one out at random.

Chuck picked up the phone, then pressed hold. 'Fay, for you,' he said.

'Yes?' Ben said, opening the file.

'The Dean doesn't want you to differentiate between credit and non-credit income on your budget. The figures you send should just be one total. And estimate your non-credit high for summer and add that in.'

'OK.'

'She said if the number of students waiting to come back to school is less than fifty per cent, never mind.'

'Never mind then,' Ben said.

'And she wants a list of non-credit activities for your programme, especially conferences.'

'Sure,' Ben said. 'I'll call back in ten minutes.'

'All they care about is keeping our income,' Chuck said. 'It'd be better not to let them have it.'

'She's supported us,' Ben said. 'What age did you get?'

'Twenty-seven.'

Ben began to type a list of activities: the children's literature conference, the video conference, the series of fiction readings.

Even if Nona could justify keeping the credit programme, he thought it would still be threatened. A degree programme shouldn't have profit and the bottom line as the final word. It shouldn't have to be so large. To develop art, a certain discretion was involved. The programme should be smaller. The faculty should be full-time. The non-credit should be limited. Daryl shouldn't be over any of it. In Lifelong Learning, the more money something made, the more successful it was considered to be.

Wasn't the real quality in how the students wrote? What they learned? Their experiences at State and their successes?

You have to fight her, Ben thought.

He wondered if she knew that he had met with Pilkington.

He would find out soon.

'You should go to Dallas and make money,' Chuck said. 'I would. Where does working here get you?' He didn't give Ben time to answer.

11

The Interview

Glancing out the window of the plane, Ben only saw the wing and the runway. He snapped the seat-belt closed and pulled the Americana Airline Magazine from the fabric pouch on the back of the seat in front. He turned a slick, coloured page, then looked up.

An hour later he sat, an unopened novel on his legs. Instead of reading, he sipped a light beer and tried to enjoy himself. What was he doing flying to Dallas to discuss a job in business? Nothing was predictable. He yawned, taking his ease the rest of the flight.

He had worked for Howard Israel nearly ten years before on a company history. Howard had had a large suite in a smoky glass office overlooking downtown Dallas. His success was apparent, but Ben quickly became more interested in characteristics of Howard's that outweighed the material advantages.

Howard spoke to him openly, and wanted to talk about his life. He smoked cigars and wore a thick beard. He drank sherry, his voice not faltering over the most intimate details he told. They had met weekly, about a book Howard was writing. The book concerned all aspects of his company that had become successful.

Being so honest from the first had involved him and Howard in a situation like a mine field. They were, after all, in it together. To step roughly on any wrong topic could explode something in their faces. What they were doing, Ben thought, was finding out what each thought about the other's problems . . . learning how to support each other. And they came to respect each other like veterans.

'You know the history of the company,' Howard said. 'For the past two years what I've talked about for twenty has started to happen.' The inside of the Mercedes was silver and luxurious. Ben looked along the highway for the familiar signs as they drove into Dallas. He could just glimpse the skyline. It certainly had changed. Howard pointed to the right at the enormous new buildings they passed. He switched to the right lane of the freeway. 'You've heard of Los Colinas?'

Ben nodded.

Howard puffed on the cigar, rolled down the window, and tossed it out.

'I have.' Ben didn't recognize any of the two – three – no, five highrise office buildings in front of him. They flashed by, and the road turned to vacant land.

'A few years ago, just before the boom, I began to make heavy investments in office property. I told you some of it. Shortly after that, some of the wealthiest men in Dallas decided to make substantial investments in hometown real estate. That's what you're looking at.'

'It looks like an enormous amount of money,' Ben said.

'It is. Billions of dollars.'

Ben took a deep breath and let it out. The investment seemed to be working.

'I'll drive by the buildings we own,' Howard said. 'They're all north of LBJ. You won't recognize the area. Even out by the university where there was nothing but pasture.'

'Do you miss Holly?' Ben asked. Holly was Howard's ex-wife who hadn't been very good to him.

'Not for a minute. I told you I wouldn't.'

'And you see the kids a lot?'

'Right now I have a court suit to see Ellen more. Did I tell you that? Holly does everything she can to keep me from it.'

Ben watched the luminous speedometer move as Howard

turned on to the north freeway. 'You know she does it because she still loves you,' Ben said.

'No,' Howard said.

'Because she's hurt. She may make a lot of money herself, but she loves you.'

'Carolyn loves me,' Howard said.

'She loves you, too. You've got good taste in women.'

'The highrise you see ahead is one of my buildings,' Howard said. 'I own about sixty per cent of it now. We had the company headquarters there until October.'

'Are we getting off?' Ben watched them pass the exit.

'The other three are in North Dallas Center. Do you want to go to the house first?'

'I'd like to stop for a drink.' The glare of the sun made Ben feel like there wasn't much air outside the car. He loosened his tie, unbuttoned his shirt collar. Ahead were – Ben began to count – nearly a dozen huge buildings, all of them impressive. 'I haven't seen the Galleria.' Ben said. 'Is that it?' Below them, the stores were clustered with crowded parking lots.

Howard signalled and waited in the line of cars just at the last exit. The road led to an unfinished intersection with a red light.

'I don't have anyone here that I can talk to,' Howard said. 'They're not in touch with themselves the way you are.'

'I'm not,' Ben said. He wished he were.

'You know how you feel about things. That's more than most people do. The more I've thought about your joining me here, the more I like the idea. And it's an opportunity for you. Ever since I've known you, you've worried about money.'

'I've had to.'

'I know that.'

'And it isn't easy,' Ben said, his tone changing. He reached back and raised the leather headrest slightly.

'Writing is harder than making money,' Howard said. 'You know I still want to write a book – you can help me with it, too.'

'OK,' Ben said.

'I know a bar up here I'll stop at. Carolyn's expecting us by six. I've asked my assistant to come for dinner. She wanted to meet you.'

Ben nodded.

'Of course Carolyn is looking forward to it. There's plenty of time for meeting others later. If you want me to be more specific on salary, I will now.'

'Yeah, I do.'

'If the job works out, you can count on an immediate retainer, a salary twice yours, and moving expenses.'

Ben nodded, his eyes suddenly open wider.

Carolyn was all over the dinner – the cobalt-rimmed plates, the golden bottles of wine, the aroma of home-cooked pasta. She sat across from Ben, next to Howard's assistant Katie, laughing, all of them relaxed. The wooden table top shone as the wine did, polished with light glowing from the chandelier.

Ben took another swallow of wine. 'So you've always wanted to write?' he asked Katie. Howard had told him. He saw the embarrassment and she shook her head.

She laid down her fork, her eyes showing that she listened.

'The first thing writing does to a person is to take up all the best of his time. This creates a basic problem. You have to make money but you can't give a job the best attention. So if you've wanted to write, you've probably had a number of jobs and gone from one to the other, telling yourself that you have to get your book out.'

'I have,' Katie said. 'When I finished Brown – I had edited the *Trojan* and published stories in school – I was going to write a novel at once and live off the proceeds.'

Ben could see that she was smart. She didn't try to fit in, not even at that moment. Her hair wasn't quite combed and she was overweight, but she probably had been pretty.

'Do you like being Howard's assistant?' he asked.

'She hasn't been for that long – a few weeks.' Howard passed the white platter of home-made noodles, then right behind it, the steaks that he had barbecued. The door to the patio was still open and Ben could see the coals glowing.

'What you say is true, though,' Katie said. 'I spent one year in Boston, then I went to New York and tried to get a job in publishing. I just refused to be a secretary.'

'You should have done it. That's how you get experience in publishing.'

'Probably. After that I had a strange two years in the New York pornography scene. I – '

'That sounds very interesting.' Ben could see Howard's surprise.

'I thought so at the time. I was doing my thing and feeling very independent from everyone, especially men. I still don't regret it, but I was taken advantage of.'

'Were you in movies?' Ben asked.

'I wrote some. None of it was professional. But I thought I was doing something that I wanted to do.'

He was right. She must have been pretty. He noticed the small nose, the plump cheeks, the lips oval.

'I learned how to get satisfaction from a man and not just lie there,' she said.

'I had to learn that, too,' Caroline said.

'I was afraid to look at a man's body when I left Brown. Like I was doing something wrong. I changed.'

'Good for you,' Carolyn said.

'Believe me, I have desires just like a man does.'

Ben held his tongue a minute.

'Don't you get tired of pretending you don't have to feel anything?' Carolyn said. 'Howard and I went through that.'

Howard's expression was immediate and he glanced away from the table.

'I just don't stay in relationships long.' Katie began to wind the white noodles around her fork. 'With Carl it's different because it's lasted a year. But I feel guilty about not telling him the truth about me. I want to be entirely honest, but it might hurt our relationship. Do you think it would?'

Her smile surprised Ben. 'I want to tell him about relationships I've had just like he tells me.'

'I'm sure it would,' he said. 'I'd care a lot.'

'The truth shouldn't hurt anything.'

'Ben's right. It does sometimes, Katie, even if it shouldn't,' Carolyn said.

Katie shook her head, agreeing, her mouth full.

'You shouldn't tell him anything.' Carolyn's voice was sympathetic.

'I just don't understand men,' Katie said.

'You sure don't.' Howard's voice was louder than polite. 'Unless you two are trying to be a turn-off.'

'Am I a turn-off, honey? Would you tell me that later tonight?'

'Women shouldn't talk like truck drivers,' Howard said.

'See – honesty just won't work with men. I don't know what they think we are. Just because I was honest.'

'You know what you should tell your boyfriend?' Ben asked. Ben could see that Howard was now rather enjoying the red wine in his glass. 'Tell him honestly how you feel about him – if you love him. If a girl told me about her sex life, I'd think it was because she didn't want me.'

'You're a chauvinist. Isn't he, Katie?'

'I'm listening. I know I'm doing something wrong.'

'You're doing a lot wrong if you're trying to attract him,' Howard said.

'I guess I just can't be honest.'

'Howard, can we show Ben the pictures of our wedding?' Carolyn asked. 'If you want – '

'I'd like to see them,' Ben said. He stood up, taking his glass with him.

'Who wants something else to drink?' Howard leaned over, to the crystal bottles on top of the bar. 'Brandy?'

'I'll take some,' Katie said. She switched to the sofa where Ben sat, her legs under her, on the floor. She looked up at Ben and began. 'I can really talk to you,' she said. 'I've told you things that almost no one knows.' She reached up, touching her forehead, her fingernails very short and her fingers pudgy. 'I don't go around telling people about my life,' she said.

She brushed her hair back with her fingers. 'I guess I cause a lot of my own problems in trying to make my life interesting.' But she wanted to decide things herself, and she had made little off judgements that kept her missing the boat.

'Howard talks about you a lot,' she said. 'All the interesting men like you and Howard are already married.' She looked up, taking a drink from Howard. 'I shouldn't have another one. I have to drive home.'

'I have the projector ready. Is it all right to turn out the lights?'

'Honey – start with those the night before. OK?'

'I already have.' He flipped the switch.

Ben crossed his legs, leaned back and watched the colourful screen. He yawned. The leather sofa was comfortable despite the puckers. He closed his eyes a second. Then he was purposely very still. He could feel Katie's head leaning against his leg, using it for a pillow.

'Honey, Phil was so funny!'

'He had just gotten in from China. That's why he's wearing the hat.'

Ben moved his toes around in his stiff brown shoes. He looked down and saw Katie's hand resting on the sofa cushion. Was she expecting him to take it? She looked about thirty-five. He thought she could be older. Not forty, he thought. He was surprised at some of the things he felt. Like they were out of the book he had read. Maybe he should take her back into the bedroom and without a word begin to unbutton the thin blouse, pull up the skirt and put his finger along the elastic panties, bringing them down, then off. He put his mouth on the nipples, the breasts large enough to be wide and soft in his hands . . .

Katie giggled and he laughed, his eyes closed. He sniffed the brandy each time before he took a sip. The smell made his eyes water and he drank, his hand softly touching Katie's hair. She put her fingers on his.

The den where they ate had sculptures on special shelves. Beyond them, the lights in the yard glowed around a fountain Ben had seen earlier, and the fountain led down several steps to a terrace and pool. He could just see the blue lights along the roof of the pool house.

He liked the money.

He blinked when the bright lights came on.

'You were asleep,' Carolyn said. 'I'm sorry. Howard – '

'Just the last minute,' Ben said. He sat up and laid the pillow back on the seat.

'I should go,' Katie said. 'I hate staying longer than I should.'

Ben listened for Carolyn to say no. She said nothing and began to collect the drinks.

'Let me help you,' Katie said.

'No. I know you have to get up early. I'm not going to do them.'

Katie smoothed back her hair, then reached down and picked up her purse from the sofa. 'I enjoyed the evening, people,' she said.

'I was glad to meet you,' Ben said. 'Send me some of your work if you ever want to.'

'I'd be too embarrassed.'

'I'd like to read it.'

'I might.' She put her arm through the shoulder strap. 'I just might.' She hugged back, quickly.

Ben watched her hurry through the entrance, the polished double doors closing slowly.

Ben walked to the open door and went out on to the patio to look at the sky. He breathed in and out, the stars above bright. He turned around, hearing Howard. 'Ben, would you like a drink?'

'I'll just sit here.' Ben yawned, looking out at the lights in the yard. A creek several hundred feet below marked the dividing line to the multi-storeyed house next door. Ben tried to imagine owning that house, the bright lights opening room after room. Instead, he thought of the expensive rent on their small house in Santa Monica.

All they could afford was a one-bedroom apartment.

The terrace was beautiful with cream wrought iron and green cushions, blue umbrellas, and heavy rust pots of flowers set along the back floor. He glanced up at Howard.

'I appreciate your asking me here,' Ben said.

Howard was sipping brandy from the snifter. 'We've known each other ten years now, and I was just thinking, this is a kind of celebration. Ten years ago next month you began working for me. What better way to celebrate than your coming to Dallas. I couldn't have been sure of my own future then.'

'I would have been,' Ben said. 'But you had a lot of changes to face. You even added to them.' He thought it showed as much about life as it did about Howard. There they both had been – Ben in another personal financial crisis and Howard, fleeing his unhappy marriage and a depressed economy. There were no easy solutions.

It had all been all right, if only they had known. It is now, Ben thought.

'I gladly have put that part of my life behind me. I don't have to worry about certain things – material ones anyway. It's a good feeling. Do you mind if I light this?' Howard took a cigar and lighter out of his pocket.

Ben motioned that he didn't mind.

Howard nodded, the cigar tip glowing.

For a moment, neither spoke.

'I was just thinking about my years of high school,' Howard spoke louder. 'My mother insisted they send me to a military school – a boarding school. I remember the teachers in that school very well. They were all unhappy.' Howard had only mentioned boarding school once.

Howard puffed, smoke billowing out. 'I think my mother and father were having some problems,' he said. 'I begged Mother not to make me go. Dad always did what she wanted. It caused me problems that I had to work out when I was grown.'

'What kind of problems?' Ben asked.

'I was mixed up emotionally. I needed to be with my grandfather and he died while I was in school there. I took his death very hard.'

'Did you have any friends?' Ben asked. 'Did you tell anyone?'

'I remember dreams that I had there – nightmares that continued through my college years.'

'What were they about?' Ben asked.

'About my identity. Who I was and what was happening in my life. A lot of it wasn't clear to me, either. I guess I had kind of a personal crisis that I haven't had since.'

Ben said nothing. He looked at Howard in the face.

'It was the most difficult period of my life. I've never told anyone but Carolyn about it. I had this teacher who taught physics. He was our dorm adviser, too. He had a one-room apartment with a kitchen and his own bath. There were four of us to a room.'

Ben listened quietly, rubbing his eyes.

'One night I had a very bad nightmare and the teacher took me to his apartment. He told me I could stay there.' He flicked ash on to the patio, then puffed, the cigar smell heavy. 'I talked to him for hours, telling him everything.'

'And you were friends with the teacher after that?'

'I never talked to him again. The next morning I found out

that my grandfather had died. I wanted to leave the school but I couldn't. I didn't have anyone to turn to.'

Howard took another deep breath then spoke louder. 'I'll show you the property tomorrow. When do you want to get up?'

'When you do,' Ben said.

'You remember what Bill did. He handled our publicity and advertising. You could handle it easily.'

Ben thought he could.

'The job's yours if you want to come,' Howard said.

Ben nodded. At that moment he wanted to tell Howard yes. 'I'd like to think about it,' he said. It was all a matter of friendship.

'Howard,' Carolyn said at the patio door. 'Are you ready to go to sleep?'

'I'll lock it when I come in,' Ben said. 'I'll sit here longer if I can. I enjoyed the dinner, Carolyn.'

'You want us to keep you company?' Carolyn walked on to the terrace. She looked tired.

'I'm enjoying it,' Ben said. 'You two go on to bed.'

'All right,' Howard said. He got up.

The glass door shut and an air conditioning vent close by clicked on. Wasn't it curious, Ben thought, that people had different experiences in life. It sounded obvious. But wasn't one of the biggest questions about life why we were born individuals?

Howard had had that trauma that Ben hadn't even imagined. And Howard had this pot of money – it had to be enormous. To run the house alone, much less the buildings and still get the other investments. While he, on the other hand, taught and worked in a college.

Why didn't money and experience drop in on him? It appeared to drop in on people. Why were some people just filthy with success?

You can own a home like this. Drive any car. Have money like water flushing through your bank.

Oh my God.

He closed his eyes, still feeling the wine.

They could own a big house in Dallas. They would travel. The money would have an importance just as the lack of it did now.

Would it buy any difference in me? he wondered. He hadn't thought of *how* he should be for a long time. Hadn't he thought most about it in school, college and even at the start of teaching?

He had quit thinking of *what* he should be, and he had become something. He felt an enormous disappointment with the idea. His life was a whole matter of what he *could* be, what decisions and work he could do – not to change himself, but to take advantage of chances.

Listen to yourself, he thought. Are *you* what questions and makes goals and decides things inside yourself?

Yes.

He could hear the stream flowing because the house had gotten so quiet and the air conditioner had shut off. Millions of dollars would mean nothing unless he decided certain things for himself first.

He was having a mid-life crisis.

He wanted money.

He saw the balcony, the flagstone and back terraces, the quiet smell of money that grew the flowers and the new kitchens, the sports cars, Cadillacs, the easy-to-look-at things.

It was the opportunity that mattered.

Ben wished that Alice were with him.

He was glad he had come to Dallas. He should thank Howard.

Disneyland

Tuesday afternoon, back in Los Angeles, Ben was in a bad
mood, waiting for Wednesday. He would now meet with Peel
at two p.m. in the President's office. He glanced in the rearview mirror at Adie and Jules, then across at Alice. He saw the
large Disneyland sign and turned left, just making the green
light.

'We're here!' Alice said. 'There it is.'

'That's Disneyland, Adie.' Jules pointed out the window
beside him.

'I know,' Adie said.

'We're going to have a lot of fun if we can find a place to
park,' Ben said. Automobiles flooded the lot. He had not
expected so many. Did all these people really have so much
fun? Ben glanced in the rearview mirror at the cars behind
him. Oh no, he thought, knowing it was his idea to come. He
hated lines.

What if at that moment, he opened his mouth, looked at
Alice and said that he *dreaded* going? The place, like church,
was already above criticism. He should be at work. He glanced
at her, then quickly away. He could tell at once that she was
worried he wouldn't enjoy it. Go ahead, her smile meant,
pretend. You won't like it one bit. I know.

He continued down a block row of cars parked in the same
direction. Not one vacant space. He pressed the brake, then
crossed to the next aisle. He had promised Jules.

From the first he wanted one thing understood – that he
would not have one moment of fun if he did not want and no

one could stop him. Even if he had suggested going, he was being dragged there, like a mule to water.

'Leave your seat belts fastened until I park,' Ben said, over the back seat. He glanced at Alice.

A tram car honked and Ben stopped to let it pick up passengers in front of them. It continued, and behind it, a blue sedan was backing out, leaving a quick vacant space. Ben pulled up and parked. He turned off the ignition.

'Just a second,' he said, making sure that Jules's hands weren't in the way as he opened the door. He got out, then pushed his seat up for them. 'I want you two to be careful all day,' he said. 'All right? Will you behave?' He unfastened both seat belts and lifted them out, Adie first.

'Uh huh,' Jules said.

'All right,' Adie said.

He held Jules's hand and Jules held Adie's as they crossed the asphalt lot. 'Honey, will you buy the tickets?' he asked.

He didn't want to know how much it cost. He waited for Alice to pay, then the four of them went through the turnstiles.

'This way,' Ben said, taking them into the main thoroughfare. 'Don't run. Wait.' He reached down and tied the undone laces on one of Jules's red striped sneakers.

Straight ahead a cold drink sign rose over a frontier store with a wishing well in front. Main Street. A carriage passed, the horse pulling it wearing bells. He saw an orange drink stand, a fried chicken place, a store front marked saloon. 'We're going to the rides first,' Ben said, unfolding the map.

The whole place was obvious like a firecracker. He realized that the second he saw it. Just past the snack stand, he could see the amusements, lines jumping up and down with children.

'Want to see the pirate ship?' he asked. He held his finger on it while he got his bearings. It should be half-way across the park, but in what direction?

'No. That.' Jules pointed to a boat ride.

'You don't mind waiting in line?' he asked.

'Please, Daddy.'

'All right.'

'Carry me.'

'Already?' He stopped, picked up Jules in one arm and Adie in the other.

'They're too heavy,' Alice said.

'No, they're not.' Ben walked just fast enough for Alice to have to hurry, too.

Money was talking everywhere. As he walked, Ben raised his eyebrows. He had not expected Disneyland to be such a *business*.

'Can we get candy?' Jules asked.

'Definitely not yet.' He set them down at the end of the line at the boat ride. The little boats in front circled pleasantly, like leaves in a current of water. Ben held up Jules so that he could see over the heads of the adults in front.

'You can drive it by yourself,' Ben said.

'I don't want to ride,' Jules said suddenly.

'It'll be fun.' Ben felt Jules's legs and arms stiffen.

'I do.' Adie handed Alice his jacket. 'I want to ride the boats.'

'You'll like it,' Ben whispered into Jules's ear.

'No, I won't go.' Jules's mouth pressed tight against Ben's ear and Ben set him down.

Ben took a step, as everyone in front of him did. 'You can drive it all by yourself,' he repeated. 'It's a big boy ride.' He had difficulty taking the next step, Jules's arms wrapped tightly around his leg like an octopus. 'You don't have to,' Ben said. 'We're just having fun. You don't have to do anything. I'll go with Adie.'

'No,' Jules said. 'I will.'

After a minute, the girl in front climbed into a boat and Jules let go of Ben. 'I'm before Adie,' he said. 'I'm first, Daddy. Wait!'

'You can both go at the same time.' Ben picked him up and

began to whisper. 'You be polite to your guest. You can't always be first.'

Adie climbed down into a boat and was carefully strapped in by the attendant. Then he let Jules down.

Jules got into a yellow boat, his teeth showing behind his grin. He did look bigger. He raised his arms, then, the seat belt ready, he pressed on the accelerator. Jules waved 'bye as the boat glided, following Adie's red boat.

For a moment, the laughter was from children, not loudspeakers. He could hear Jules and Adie, their faces pantomiming, their smiles like toys.

The whole place was the most expensive toy store in the world. Ben saw Jules turned around, waving. He liked anything that Jules enjoyed. 'They must be making a fortune,' Ben said. 'Look at the lines.'

'I loved it when I was eight,' Alice said. 'I didn't mind them. Over there – the GE building was new the first time my grandfather brought me. It has – '

'So GE rents it from Disney?' Ben asked. 'And pays for the display people pay Disney to see?' Did Disney make money on rent from the exhibits and from tickets? If so, it was a great business. He glanced at his watch. It would be at least five before they could go. They would be starting home at the height of traffic. Alice didn't answer and waved at the kids. He opened the map. If they were at the boat ride, then the pirate ship should be to his right. He shielded his eyes with his palm.

'I loved it,' Alice said again. 'I bet Jules does.'

Ben stood a moment, bored. Restless. He was frowning and pretending that the sun made him squint. It didn't. She didn't look like she was even paying attention to what he was thinking. Shouldn't he and Alice be talking about his job, L.A., looking for a house, what she wanted? What they were going to do. Ben bit his lip and looked in the opposite direction. He turned back.

'I need to call the office in a minute,' he said.

'You can now.'

'I will in a minute.'

'OK,' Alice said, her face happy.

Ben frowned.

'You can go ahead and call and I'll watch them,' Alice said.

'All right.'

Ben walked across to a row of pay telephones outside a snack bar. He dropped in a quarter and carefully dialled his number at the office. Chuck would answer it.

'Hello,' he said.

'Just a minute,' Chuck said. 'Can you hold, please?'

Ben hesitated. 'Yes.' The hold button made a noise and the line sounded dead. He waited.

'I'm sorry. I had to go into your office,' Chuck whispered. 'Are you at Disneyland?'

'I said I would be.'

'There was no place to call you. Daryl came in an hour ago and said he wanted all our financial files. I told him I had to ask you.'

'Good.'

'He said I had to show him where they were.'

'That's OK,' Ben said. 'You shouldn't fight him. Did you show him?'

'He took all of them into his office. He has Corrine making copies. He wants me to make a list of faculty salaries this term.'

'Is he there now?'

'No. I'll quit if he comes back in. I won't work for him.'

'I'll talk to him,' Ben said. 'You did the right thing.'

'I mean it,' Chuck said. 'I'll quit.'

'It's all right,' Ben said. He hung up. Daryl was searching for anything that looked like an expense. He didn't understand how Ben cut costs. He gave the faculty small luxuries and asked them to accept a low budget that made the whole programme stronger. He cared about how the faculty and staff felt. Free parking or dinners at the faculty club – small personal attentions were worth many times what they cost. Ben had been able to lower expenses everywhere by paying attention to detail and giving at the right places. If Daryl started cutting at the wrong places, the income would suffer, people would quit, the image would fall, and expenses would soar.

Daryl had no right to the files without asking him first.

Ben put in another quarter and dialled. 'Corrine,' he said. 'Can I talk to Daryl?'

'You sound mad,' she said.

'Is he in?'

'He's on the phone.'

'I'll call back,' Ben said. He hung up.

On the sidewalk a tiny parade of a giant Mickey Mouse, Donald Duck and Pluto passed. Parents quickly pointed them out to the children. The balloon figures were carried on stilts, and actors in bright makeup hugged everyone. The characters continued and Ben saw Jules waving at him.

Jules turned the wheel wildly, the boat running along a curved rail underneath the shallow water.

Ben wished he could go back to the office and meet Daryl face to face.

'Is something wrong?' Alice asked.

'It's Daryl,' Ben said. 'Never mind. I have to call back in a minute.'

'Daddy!' Jules said, his boat coming up to unload. Jules got out then reached up for Ben to carry him. Ben picked him up, and waited for Alice to carry Adie. 'Would you two like something to eat?'

'Yes,' Adie said.

'A hot dog.'

Ben shifted, holding Jules higher. He wove through the crowd quickly. He stopped at a soft drink stand and stood in line, looking at the painted menu. 'I just want something to drink,' Alice said.

'Would you like a hamburger, Adie?' Ben asked. He didn't want anything to eat. Neither did Jules finally. Ben shifted, scooting Jules up higher. Jules bent over farther. He made a sudden sound in his throat, from his stomach. Ben felt something run down his neck and fall on to his back. He turned around, seeing Jules's pale cheeks. Jules threw up more, surprising them both.

The woman behind in line stepped back, quickly. 'He got too excited,' Alice said.

Ben set Jules down and taking his hand, walked away from the line. He took his arms out of his coat and squatted. He put his palm against Jules's forehead. 'How do you feel?' he asked.

'Fine.'

'Come rest a minute.' Ben folded his coat and laid it on the bench beside Adie. 'Jules doesn't feel well,' he said. 'Come here.' He set Jules on his lap, his face against his arm. 'In a minute you'll be OK,' Ben said.

'I'm OK now.'

'Rest a minute, then we'll go to the pirate ship.'

Ben went to the rest room, took off his shirt and cleaned up.

He came back in a better mood. Didn't he want to throw up, too?

'OK,' he said. He took the map out of his back pocket and spread it against a bench. 'Look. We're going here.' He pointed to the drawing of the pirate ship. 'Do you want to see the pirate ship?'

'Yes!' Adie said.

'Come on!' Jules said, pulling on his hand.

Ben led them along the crowded lane to the ship.

'Let me take them,' Alice said. 'You call them and we'll meet you back here in a few minutes.'

'All right,' Ben said. He watched them disappear, then found a telephone.

He dialled quickly and told Corrine he wanted Daryl.

'Sure thing, honey,' she said.

'Hello?' Daryl said.

Ben could have exploded. He stood, feeling the anger in his voice. 'I understand you went into my office and took out files,' Ben said.

Daryl said nothing.

'If you want something from our files, you ask me. I want to make one thing perfectly clear – '

'Yes?'

'I won't let you push me around. If I were you, I wouldn't try.'

'I asked for you and you were out of the office.'

'You should have waited.'

'I want to meet with you. Already I've found a number of expenses to cut. Just as I expected. And I'm going to evaluate classes. I've set up a meeting with you for tomorrow afternoon. I don't want to discuss anything over the phone.'

'I don't want to discuss anything at all. And how can you cut Danz when he's ten times the administrator you are?' Ben waited for an answer. He stood a moment, hearing the music from another parade. Then he hung up. He saw a giant Dumbo, a Goofy, a Donald Duck.

He had to tell Peel that he would not work with Daryl one more week. Everything Daryl was doing was negative and Nona backed him. Ben looked a minute at the telephone. The programme had to be moved. There was no question of it. They would not let a successful programme alone.

He sighed, rubbing his forehead. Now, try to have fun, he thought, for the kids. You're being unpleasant. And everyone else is having fun. Wasn't that a good place to start having fun – because everyone else was? He guessed not. He could see them just coming out and he waved, pointing to the next ride.

Four hours and a half later, they got into the Honda, and unloaded the souvenirs they had bought. Ben got the pillows from the floorboard and gave one to Jules and to Adie. 'Lie down on them,' he said. 'Get comfortable; we've got a long trip.' He pushed up the visor, settled in the seat, turned on the ignition. He could see in the rearview mirror that they had already closed their eyes. Ben started out of the parking lot, in line.

The traffic was heavy on the streets leading to the freeway. Ben joined it, coming up to the entrance. Then he saw ahead – the stopped cars, jammed as if Los Angeles were being evacuated. He signalled quickly. 'Let's get something to drink and wait it out,' he said, his voice relieved.

Alice was glad to. 'Let's do,' she said.

He pressed on the gas, hurrying right and turned into a parking lot for a bowling alley. Up close he saw a sign on the door. He stopped the car. *Closed for renovation*. The place was closed. The cars in the lot were parked while people had shared rides to work. The traffic just across on the freeway was like rushing water, knee deep and he couldn't plunge in. He turned off the ignition. 'We have to wait,' he said. Adie and Jules were asleep. He thought about Disneyland and about waiting and he closed his eyes, trying not to complain. He could see that Alice was right. He should have known he wouldn't like it.

He felt nervous, thinking of meeting with Peel.

University Politics

The red sofa was the colour of Chancellor Peel's tongue, the white lamp like his hair, the pale blue carpet like the watery eyes. Ben sat in Peel's office, uncomfortable, his easy smile waiting for Peel to end a telephone conversation.

Peel's voice was deeper than most people's, the expression larger than life-like, the hand he finally put out stronger and bigger than Ben's. 'I'm sorry about the telephone,' he said.

Ben would have agreed with almost anything and have run away if he could have. Left Peel with a good impression and have gone outside for air.

'Ben,' Peel said, slowly, 'I understand your situation.'

Ben cleared his throat. 'What I want is not just for me. I want to be sure what I believe should happen to the programme will.'

'I understand that.' Peel crossed his legs and lit a cigarette without taking his eyes from Ben's.

'I want . . . the programme under someone other than Nona. She has strengths, certainly.' Ben risked looking him directly in the face. 'I admire her. But she doesn't understand what the programme needs. She's concerned with Continuing Ed, which she well should be.' He wanted to glance at his watch, but he didn't. He returned the smile he saw, his worry making him breathe heavily. 'I want the programme moved out of the School of Lifelong Learning.'

Peel nodded seriously, his eyebrows higher. 'I understand. It should be.'

'I have another offer,' Ben said lowly.

Hesitation. Then, another slow nod. 'There are key committees that need new leadership,' Peel said. 'I can see you contributing to them. I hope you're not considering another position.'

'If a programme can't have quality, then it doesn't have a place in the university,' Ben said. 'And the school itself is blocking the development of the programme. I could tell you details of what I've been dealing with.'

'I know. If you will give me until fall, I can assure you. You've probably heard about my conflict with Nona already.'

'I trust you,' Ben said. 'But I can't work with Daryl – '

Peel crossed his legs, the white suit pressed, the shoes bright. He wore a thick gold watch. Ben looked at the wide grey brows, the ruddy cheeks, the white teeth, the expensive tie. 'If you could give me until September, I could promise you now what I would do then,' Peel said. 'I am sure that more reorganization will come next fall. You know that Nona has plans for retiring. When she does, there will be a natural time for change.'

'I understand that.'

'It would avoid unpleasantness. I promised her that there would be no more changes this spring. To do so now would be difficult.' He nodded again. 'You can give me certain things – a little time.'

'I have two weeks to decide on the offer that I have in Dallas. I'll stay if the programme can be moved.' Ben could see that Peel wanted the programme moved. Do it, he thought. You have the power at your fingertips.

'I'm sure it can be,' Peel said. 'Say you were to join another department and announce that you are starting a new writing programme.' Peel looked away, toward the window. 'That would create a constitutional crisis since the university can't have two identical programmes. The degree committee would have to be called and – ' He hesitated. 'Perhaps the old programme could be declared dead for one minute, and in the next, the new one could take over.'

Ben nodded, startled. What? he thought. He imagined Nona during these events. Use your power, you're President. Everyone is afraid of you. Are you afraid of her?

'Of course that was off the top of my head,' Peel said. 'I will have to think about how. I'd appreciate your confidence about this. If Nona were to hear –'

'I won't tell anyone.'

'Then we can work something out.'

Ben was surprised.

'Please don't accept anything else meanwhile.'

'I won't.' Ben sat a moment, then spoke. 'I don't mean to create a problem for you. I understand that you don't want to deal with this so quickly.'

'It's all right. I'll call you at ten in the morning.'

'Thank you, then.' Ben stood, his footprints in the thick carpet, and a moment later the heavy oak door closed, air conditioning making the dark hallway cold.

He was almost sure that the programme would be moved. He walked into the hallway. He was surprised at the quality the higher administration had at State. He couldn't help but grin. He had washed his hands of Daryl. Imagine what Nona would say, he thought.

He had to pick George up at the airport.

Three p.m. He left the building and went to the top floor of parking garage number three. He watched carefully driving down, then exited on Stephens Street, taking the freeway. He continued toward the airport, hoping the traffic wouldn't be terrible.

It was, but he found a place to park in front of Delta. He crossed over the median, bringing a history of the S.S. to read in the lobby while he waited for George's flight. As he entered the terminal, he stood before a televised flight schedule and looked across to see George coming toward him.

'Ben,' George said. He already was carrying his bags. 'I got an earlier flight. I just tried to call. You were in a meeting.'

Ben reached down to pick up one of the brown bags. 'Come on,' he said.

'Could we get a quick drink?' George asked. He motioned to a sign indicating the bar.

Ben walked fast behind him, glad. He would have a strong scotch.

Forty minutes later they walked out of the terminal and waited for the courtesy vans and automobiles to pass before they crossed the median. The sky overhead was dulled with smog. Ben entered the parking garage and pointed to his car. 'I hope you don't mind my complaining,' he said. He had told George everything. He set down the canvas bag and took out the car key.

As he raised the hatchback, he leaned over, giving George a hug. 'I'm glad you're here,' he said. 'It helps our image to bring you in to talk.'

'Look at that smog,' Ben said. He got in. He waited for George, then started the engine and began backing from the space.

'New York has smog, too.'

'Not like this?'

'No. But you don't have the subway. When I go out in the evenings now I take a taxi back. I don't trust it any more at night.'

'You don't have to drive in the traffic anyway.' Ahead, cars were lined at the entrance to Airport Boulevard. The air in the distance was even dirtier. Like all of L.A. had sinus trouble. Ben put the car in neutral and waited, his elbow resting on the open window edge. He gave a left signal, hoping to change lanes. 'You know how difficult it would be to pull a programme quickly,' Ben said.

'It would be impossible at my university,' George said. 'I think you should be willing to give them a little time.'

'He said he would probably do it,' Ben said. 'I'll know in the morning.'

'Then he will. Give him a chance to do what he can.' George stretched, loosening his silk tie. 'It's good to be in California. Tell me, how is Jules? I've got him a present from F.A.O. Schwartz in my suitcase. And since we have nothing planned tonight, I'm taking Bob Masselink and his wife to dinner at eight.'

'You've saved Friday night?'

'I have. And I'm going to polish my head for Jules.'

'And use peanut butter to keep on your moustache. Look at that – ' Ben pressed on the gas, entering Airport. He stopped quickly, in heavy traffic.

'I was ready for a change of scene,' George said. 'You know what people call Manhattan? "The Winner's Circle". And they're right. It gets more expensive each year. Especially the last three. And the new construction has brought more congestion to the Village. You should have seen some people's faces when I told them I was to spend a week in sunny California. To give two talks, get some sun and enjoy friends.'

'Your apartment is ready,' Ben said. 'Everything is.' He saw the traffic clearing quite a bit just ahead. He glanced at the dashboard, surprised. He sped up to fifty-five. He had asked Chuck to leave a bottle of iced champagne in the living room.

'Don't be in a hurry to decide anything,' George said. 'They are being fair with you.'

'I won't. I'll come by in the morning after I talk with Peel. OK?'

'I'll be up,' George said. 'We will celebrate.' He leaned back, the liquor he'd had, red on his cheeks. 'Thank you Ben,' he said, 'for bringing me out here.'

The engine whined as Ben changed lanes, speeding past the right row of cars.

He had better stop by the office before he went home. He almost felt like whistling. After he helped George with the two suitcases, he walked across campus to the brick building.

Chuck was typing fast with two fingers, the keys typing like bullets. 'Howard Israel called,' he said.

'What time?'

'An hour ago. He said he'd call back.'

'Please tell him I'll call him tomorrow, and thank him for calling.' Ben sat down on one of the office chairs, relaxed. He looked up when he heard the door open.

Daryl held several white sheets and looked surprised when he saw Ben.

Does he know? Ben wondered.

'These new guidelines are from Nona,' Daryl said. 'They list new rules for all expenditures.' His sleeves were rolled up and he looked tired around his brown eyes. 'I'll be glad to discuss any of them with you.'

Ben nodded. 'That's fine.'

Daryl sat down on the wooden chair beside him. 'I'll give you a couple of days to go over them. Meanwhile, if you can, tell me the minimum you need for promotion next year by tomorrow afternoon.'

Ben shook his head yes.

'I can't promise you anything, but we can try.'

'No problem.'

'And I'd like to talk with you tomorrow about Chuck. I'd rather not go into it now.'

'All right.'

Daryl was pleased. 'I know we've had our problems,' he said, 'but you and I know how to get along. I have no complaints about your programme. I've told Nona that. You and I have worked together much better the past few days.'

Ben didn't ask why.

'We still have to lower the seven thousand you said you needed this term.'

'There is forty-five thousand in the accounts.'

'No. Nona has authorized a transfer.' He handed Ben the pages, then turned to leave. He left the door open, the heels of his shoes noisy in the hallway.

Ben put the papers on the desk in the file basket. He went

into his office, sat down, and felt uncomfortable in the high back chair. He wondered if he should call Howard back. What could he tell him for sure. He was grateful, regardless . . . So they would transfer the amount in his accounts without even asking him. Don't get angry, he thought. Tomorrow you won't answer to them. They will have to give the money back.

He locked his office and hurried down the stairs to the lobby, then through the glass door that shut automatically. The light was bold. He noticed the last person he wanted to see. Nona. She walked toward him, her expression concerned. It was too late for him to avoid her.

He quickly guessed that she didn't know he had spoken with Peel. She was over her head in work, her face long, her expression too busy to waste time.

He wouldn't have been surprised if she had blurted something out that he would have to face. Ben thought about her bronchitis. 'Is your throat better?' he asked, waiting and holding open the door for her.

'No.' She stopped outside on the porch.

He let the door close. 'You've got to rest your voice if you're going to get well,' he said. It was true. Up close she looked feverish, her grey eyes red.

'Just when can I?' She cleared her throat, it obviously burning. 'I haven't even had lunch. I'm not lucky like you. There's no one home to take care of me when I'm sick.'

He was surprised she was ever sick. He thought he might like to know why she had never married, but he thought he knew. Who after all would be willing to take the back seat to all her responsibilities? She wasn't giving up any. But she was feminine, her expression almost daring him to be more personal.

'Are you going to see Daryl?'

'No.' Her mouth tightened. 'I did want to tell you before you meet with Daryl about it, that he and I spoke about Chuck. Daryl says Chuck is rude and often absent from the office. I told him to cut that position in your programme if he thought it possible, but to talk with you first. It wasn't his idea.'

Ben thought about Peel quietly. He had been right to go around her.

'You don't have to agree,' she said. 'You're a good administrator. You've done well. I'm sorry to make you angry, but nothing can be done about the budget.'

Yes it can, he thought. You're going to have to cut your losses. Keep Danz, fire Daryl. Cut every programme that is losing and will continue to. Don't ruin what works.

He indicated to her that he would talk to Daryl about Chuck.

'I've asked,' she said, 'that all new expenditures over $50 be countersigned by Daryl. I'm depending on his advice.' She coughed, then took a kleenex from her suit pocket. 'It won't do any good to argue with him,' she said. She started inside, and Ben held open the door, watching her heavily climb the stairs. He was puzzled how Daryl could be so persuasive with her. Was it sexual? Regardless, he had gone around them.

The Phone Call

Ten a.m.

Ben sat in his office, waiting for Peel's call.

The programme would be inestimably better off moved.

He thought of what he would do. Develop tenure faculty slots. Have a whole track with an M.A. in writing for science and medicine and one for writing for law and business. Build up the money.

No more meetings with Daryl.

He would save lots of time.

He crossed his legs, and looked out the window. He would take Alice and Jules somewhere on a short vacation. He would have the summer off.

My God. He would have the *entire* summer off.

He began to smile.

Maybe he had broken free of the terrible situation he had felt. Could it be true?

He would work with a dean that he could talk to. Get back to his novel.

Had he possibly done that?

Yes.

But he still wouldn't be making enough money. Wasn't his future waiting? If he was successful, he could retire and live and write what he chose. Didn't that sound better?

He looked at his watch. Five until ten. He sat, waiting.

He picked up the phone and buzzed the inner office. 'Has Chancellor Peel called?' he asked.

'I'll put him right through when he does,' Chuck said. 'I'm waiting for him.'

'Good.' Ben hung up. He picked up a student thesis and put it back down.

He wanted to call home but didn't want to be on the line. He looked out the window.

At five after ten, he began to feel nervous.

At ten-twenty, Ben picked up the phone. He dialled carefully.

'Hello,' he said, 'this is Ben Escobio.'

'Yes, Professor Escobio.'

'Is Chancellor Peel in?'

'He is, but he's busy. He shouldn't be much longer.'

'Fine,' he said.

'I'll tell him you called. He's been with Dean Weygand over an hour now. He has another appointment at 10.30.'

'Thank you,' Ben said.

He hung up. Something was wrong. Why was Nona there?

A minute later the phone surprised him and he answered quickly. 'No problem,' he said as if it weren't.

'Nona was here at seven this morning waiting for me,' Peel said. 'Bob Masselink called her late last night and told her about our conference – which very much surprised her. I hadn't had a chance to talk with her.'

'What?'

'It seems that Bob had dinner with a friend of yours who told him the entire situation. Bob is a close friend of Nona's. I was rather embarrassed. I had made certain agreements with her that I hoped she wouldn't mind my breaking.'

Ben said nothing. Bob had had dinner with George. He was mentioned. It was his own fault for telling.

'The contrary is true. She would mind very much. I can promise that next fall – by Christmas – your programme will be moved. It's not possible at this moment. We will give you tenure and meet your salary request.'

'Yes,' Ben said. There was no negotiating now.

'I hope you will work with me,' Peel said. 'The university needs you. But I need more time, especially now.'

'Thank you,' Ben said. 'Can I call you later?'

'Of course.'

'Thank you.'

Ben hung up. He closed the blind in his office and turned off the light. He walked down the hallway, past Daryl's office, to the stairs, then outside. He hurried through the bright light to his car. He had only thought he was through with Daryl and Nona. Now, they would only be worse. It was his own fault.

15

Deciding

Ben hurried down Hollywood Boulevard, then turned left to
Sunset, passing stores, a synagogue with an imposing green
marble entrance, a fire station, the world moving as he was.
They were all on a slide, one behind the other. He straightened
the rearview mirror, then raised the sun-visor. He rolled down
the window, the sunshine strong. He passed the pink Beverly
Hills Hotel, and after a few blocks, reached UCLA. He turned
on Warren, toward Wilshire. He realized the changes he faced.
Nona would be tougher. She would sick Daryl on him, and try
to persuade him to give in. And he did not trust Peel. When he
saw the campus, he noticed the wooden sign for the Botanical
Gardens. He and Jules and Alice had gone there twice. A
garden in the middle of Westwood. He could be alone.

Ben suddenly pulled over, parked at a meter, got out and
locked the door. He put two quarters in the meter. He
followed along a path filled with gravel and lined by timber.
The entrance to the Gardens was empty and surrounded by
bamboo trees. He continued to a small green pond, its surface
as dark as the soil around it. The pond had large gold and
green fish flashing in the water. He stepped off the path into a
dense growth of short brush and tall trees. He pushed back
branches heavy with leaves. He stepped where he could see the
path, but no one from there could see him easily.

He sat on the thin briefcase he carried. Sunlight made
impressions on the dirt, shadowing leaves on branches. A bird
whistled, calling. The high voice persisted, clear, then what
was probably a smaller bird, squeaked. Ben glanced up,

hearing a buzz. The fly's wings shone, fan shaped. Ben loosened his tie then unbuttoned his shirt collar.

A spider web on the closest tree stretched wide. Strands of the web jutted to other branches. The threads were resilient, billowed slightly by a wind. A small bug was caught in them. He noticed a dried, brown leaf held by a strand of web and circling in the sunlight. Ben breathed in deeply, leaning back, his coat against the leaves, his head rested on his palms, his knuckles on the ground.

He was used to running a department, giving out jobs, admitting students. His world was circled by writers who were friends and by writing, which he cared about. His position made it possible for him to do things he liked for people.

Well, he thought, what should I do now? He closed his eyes, glad to be alone.

He wouldn't own a house – ever, if he stayed. The smog gave him bronchitis, the traffic got slower every year, and something violent could happen. It was true. He didn't think L.A. was good for Jules.

Then why stay? Wouldn't money make a difference, a clean sweep, bringing a choice of houses, cars, restaurants, clothes, anything to buy? Maybe Dallas offered more than he realized.

Or was it Los Angeles that was wrong? Should he just leave the city? It was only going to get larger and more expensive to live in. Because people loved it. L.A. offered opportunity, stars, fame. His programme would not have its best qualities in any other city. It took advantage of the opportunity, as it well should.

The difficulty wasn't really the city or teaching or the school. How did people like him who didn't make a high salary, live? The problem was economics. Every professional with his salary lived like he did. Put up with the problems and complained.

Then why not leave? Go to Dallas. Get away from being broke? He lay back, staring at a thin white cloud slowly passing.

The answer was written all over him. It was like skin. People could see it on his face. He wanted to teach. To write. He loved it for what it meant: how he could think, talk to other people, arrange his time.

Then why not stay?

The indecision made him want to groan. Or why not go to another school? Didn't that make sense? He remembered the opening at the University of Tennessee.

He raised himself up, slapped at a fly buzzing and lay back. He watched another gnat, then listened to a caw-caw-caw. Under some dry, golden magnolia leaves a thick grey web made a screen. A black beetle, light-bulb-shaped, crawled on the toe of his shoe. He reached down and flicked off the beetle.

One bird suddenly made a sound that closely resembled flicking a flint, trying a lighter. Suddenly four or five called out at once. Why were they calling? Did they all notice him?

Everything in his life was in human terms. Like groceries in the refrigerator, clothes in closets, water running through the pipes. The books he had read told him where and what everything was. His world was on the television, on the telephone, in newspapers and magazines. His life was all about *people*. Yet everything around him at this minute lived outside people most of the time. He should understand that.

He closed his eyes. The questions that he should be asking about his life had little to do with his job. He was ignoring life around him.

Wasn't he even ignoring other people? Yes, if he thought about them only in relation to himself.

He heard a jet overhead and following the noise, could just see the vapour trailing.

You enjoy teaching, he thought. But you have to leave the city. He had created a situation that made change inevitable.

The clear wings of a fly on a leaf before him had the thinnest black lines, almost like blood was in them. The fly spread them, then was gone. Ben traced it for a minute.

He lay back, his eyes on the sky. He would go some place

where the sky was clear. He could change his situation like he wanted, couldn't he?

At two o'clock, Ben walked into the house, the louvred windows open, the orange carpet swept, roses on the mantel, the dining table shiny. He could hear Alice humming in the kitchen. The room smelled of furniture polish.

'Is that you?' Alice asked. She came into the room.

He laid his briefcase on the coffee table and sat on the sofa. He saw through the window that Snowy was outside on the drive.

'How was the meeting?' Alice sat beside him, her cheeks red from working. She straightened a pillow nervously, then scooted closer.

He began to tell her what had happened. Peel had said no and it was Ben's own fault. What did she want to do? He did not want to work with Daryl any longer.

He could see Jules coming through the doorway into the living room. He saw him so small, then saw a figure in his mind, a little boy getting taller and taller. It was Jules growing up. It was still happening to Ben too.

He smelled her hair and saw the light shining on it. She put her arm around his neck. Ben leaned back, relaxing. There wasn't any other choice that he could see. He knew that she would agree.